DEVIL
TAKE
IT

DEVIL TAKE IT

DANIEL DEBS NOSSITER

Heresy Press • New York

Heresy Press books may be purchased in bulk at special discounts for sales promotion, corporate gifts, fund-raising, or educational purposes. Special editions can also be created to specifications. For details, contact the Special Sales Department, Skyhorse Publishing, 307 West 36th Street, 11th Floor, New York, NY 10018 or info@skyhorsepublishing.com.

Skyhorse Publishing® is a registered trademark of Skyhorse Publishing, Inc.®, a Delaware corporation.

Visit our website at skyhorsepublishing.com.

HERESY PRESS
P.O. Box 425201
Cambridge, MA 02142
heresy-press.com

Heresy Press is an imprint of Skyhorse Publishing.

10 9 8 7 6 5 4 3 2 1

Library of Congress Cataloging-in-Publication Data is available on file.

Jacket design by Elizabeth Cline

Print ISBN: 978-1-949846-62-1
Ebook ISBN: 978-1-949846-63-8

Printed in the United States of America

With gratitude and affection to Vicki Samakow-Sims,
friend and colleague through many drafts, and warm
thanks to Dr. Bernard Schweizer for his deft editing, this
story is for my wife Nancy and our sons, Andrew and Eric.

CHAPTER ONE

Eustace Bogges was a man of words who considered himself a man of deeds and so, emerging from the library, book in hand, he felt pleasantly resolute. He was a solid figure, thickset, not tall, with a vast belly and small feet invisible from his presently upright position. His features were broad and appealingly beastlike. He bore a strong resemblance to a benign hippo. Bogges set off with care; his awkward physical arrangement made forward motion a balancing act. He crossed Georgetown University's front lawn and glanced up at the Healy Building. He imagined the taste of the gray granite, Gothic grit between tongue and teeth. A remarkable pantomime, playing out on the grand stairway of the building, caught his attention. A gleaming black poodle, which might have been mistaken at a distance for a Great Dane, stood planted across several flights of steps in three-quarters profile to Bogges. At the top of the stairs, a priest from the Jesuit community was making shooing motions with both hands. The poodle gazed up unmoved, indifference that might have been boredom. For

a moment it turned eyes cracked and inflamed on Bogges and fixed him
with a crimson glare. Bogges seemed to hear a voice say that even a gambler
finds Hell more compelling than Las Vegas. Before he could consider this
unexpected thought, the poodle turned its gaze back on the priest. The
priest had stopped gesticulating. He proceeded to raise his right arm and
described a cross in the air.

"In Nomine Patris, et Filii, et Spiritus Sancti," he intoned.

The poodle stiffened along the length of its body. Alarming muscles
erupted through the black curls. The priest's solemn look hardened. His
outthrust jaw hung like a lantern from a courtyard wall. Then the dog
yawned and relaxed its forequarters just as if it had shrugged its shoulders.
After a longish pause it turned away, its muzzle still pointed skyward and,
parading over the lawn, marched out the O Street gate. The priest caught
sight of Bogges and again described a cross before disappearing inside.
Bogges now also made for the gate. There was no sign of the creature outside in the cobblestone street. Bogges approached a group of students. He
wondered if they'd seen the dog, wondered what kind of impression it had
left on them. They were occupied taking pictures of themselves, laughing
and comparing the self-portraits. They didn't notice or pretended not to
notice Bogges, who had to step off the curb to get around them. To distract
himself from thoughts of the unsettling dog, he turned his mind to the
present craze for auto-photographs—selfies. Why do they talk this way, he
wondered, veggies, doggies, foodies, lisping baby talk, sentimental kitsch
personas. These thoughts got him most of the way home. Only when Bogges glanced around before turning the key in his front door did he imagine
that he'd glimpsed a black poodle tail vanishing up 29th Street at the end
of the block. He locked the door after himself, slid the chain home, set
his book atop the pile of unpaid bills on the mail table, and went to the
bar cart. He mixed a martini in a tumbler and settled into the small green
rocking club chair which fitted him like a glove. Alone in his front parlor,
he looked out vaguely through the dormer window to the street. He had
spent Sunday afternoon in the customary way since his divorce from Sally Benton: a double order of Smitty's meat loaf at Martin's Tavern a few

blocks away, then a pleasant hour or two wandering the stacks of Lauinger Library a few blocks farther on from Martin's. The stacks, to Bogges, were very much like the Elysian Fields as described in ancient times; here one was free to converse with the wisest, the most charming, the most amusing of all those who have lived. One never knew quite whom one would encounter. Today he'd stumbled on a curiosity, a shelf of Bollandist publications. The Bollandists, he learned, were a Belgian Jesuit society dedicated to the scholarly study of saints and saintliness. He'd taken down a volume at random and discovered the Bollandists also interested themselves in demonology. This made sense to Bogges: what would be the use of the one without the temptations of the other. A Father Joseph de Tonquedec, SJ had written an essay titled "Nervous and Mental Illnesses and Diabolic Possession." He'd thumbed through a few pages and was struck by Father de Tonquedec's observation that "Satan's masterpiece, the great work of the master of illusion, is his present success in passing himself off as nonexistent. He has every interest in doing so."

Now, however, Bogges didn't feel like reading further. He'd somehow lost interest in the Devil. He began to muse about work and the workweek ahead. It seemed to him that passing oneself off as nonexistent had useful applications at the office; all the people one didn't want to talk to would never approach. It then occurred to Bogges that many of his colleagues were already practicing a form of passing oneself off as nonexistent, not recognizing him, or others, as they met in the corridor or riding in the elevator. This led to the further thought that perhaps the office was even more like the Devil's playground than had been apparent. His colleagues made him think longingly of the Lauinger stacks. I should have become a librarian, he told himself. Bogges's eyes began to blink. He drowsed. Like a heavily laden barge come loose from its moorings, Bogges drifted off.

He found himself in an office or study—there were books on the shelves—although the plaster-of-Paris cats preening as bookends and dividers suggested the hand of an amateur or Midwestern decorator. Dusty Venetian blinds drawn against a bright sun gave the room a black-and-white early camera light. Bogges was sitting semi-recumbent in a leather recliner before a metal desk looking up at a series of diplomas from an obscure and remote university granted to one Grippin Fall, doctor of psychiatry. Behind the desk, a tiny, sharp-faced man with a Van Dyke beard whose point drew attention to a prominent Adam's apple, wearing a soiled white dress shirt, which emphasized the personage's decisively seedy aspect, spoke.

"These things you don't like hearing about, Mr. Bogges, they include the French, the Arabs, the Chinese, Canadians and Mexicans, English and Irish, Germans and Africans, Indians both eastern and western; I believe you also said, Christians, Jews, Hindus, and Muslims, liberals and conservatives, writers, editors, actors, models, athletes, bankers and stockbrokers, blacks and whites—I've got it right so far, have I?"

"Yes, any group."

"But everybody belongs to a group of one kind or another."

"Yes, the problems of the world are mostly caused by other people. It's only made worse when they group together."

"Your objections have recently taken on a somewhat demonstrative expression."

"Some might think so."

"You feel you can't control yourself?"

"No, not at all. I could control myself if I wanted to. I don't want to anymore."

Dr. Fall made a little tent with his hands and held them out in front of his nose. "Why don't we go over the incident that prompted this visit in more detail," he suggested.

The psychiatrist drew the tent closer to his eyes, and Bogges noticed that the man's arms were curiously foreshortened, almost dwarfish. The doctor's beard reinforced the impression of a mannikin or homunculus. There was something counterfeit about him, this office, the whole setup. Nevertheless, he launched into his narrative for a second time. After all, he was paying for the doctor's abbreviated hour.

"As I told you, I'm the editor of the letters page of *The Washington Oracle*."

"An interesting job, I imagine."

Bogges grunted. "I've begun ... I mean, from time to time I contribute a letter of my own."

"Is that why the letters all sound as though they're written by the same person?"

"No, that's my editing. The letters are supposed to represent the readers' opinions, not mine."

"Then how can you edit them?"

Dr. Fall was missing the point. Bogges had an idea he was doing this willfully and, somehow, malevolently. "You don't understand. I've been writing letters under pseudonyms and publishing them as though they were from readers."

"Does this have something to do with your dislike of groups?"

Bogges hadn't thought of it this way. He didn't much like writers. He supposed it was only reasonable not to like readers. "I guess, up to a point, but what I don't like is how deadly earnest people are about their opinions. It's not just being pompous. They're trying to force their views on you, but what they're really after is getting their own way."

"Tell me, Mr. Bogges, would you say that you get annoyed when you don't get your own way, that you don't like it when things aren't going just right?"

"Only a hypocrite would deny that. On the other hand, I don't see how my getting annoyed distinguishes me from everyone else."

"And you pride yourself on not being hypocritical."

"No, that's not a matter of pride."

"But wouldn't you agree that hypocrisy is sometimes necessary, that white lies are not particularly harmful and that they're even useful to smooth relationships?"

Having scored this point, Dr. Fall gave a hypocritical little smirk.

Bogges drew a breath. "You smooth a bird's ruffled feathers or a dog's bristling fur, but people aren't birds or dogs."

"You are playing with words, Mr. Bogges. You do a lot of that, n'est-ce pas?"

Bogges became instantly alert. Since his first youthful visit to Paris, all his nightmares had begun with someone speaking French.

"Je suis aussi l'ambigu," added the doctor.

"What did you say? Why are you speaking French?"

"Calmez-vous mon bon monsieur. I merely said, á façon de parler, that life is ambiguous, doubtful, contingent. You appear to want everything cut and dried. You yourself are not so straightforward as you pretend. La volonté et l'esprit, that is everything."

"Answer my question. Why are you speaking French?" Bogges's voice was strained.

"Ça se sent, ça ne se dit pas. I'm so sorry. I did not mean to upset you. Certain thoughts can best be expressed in the language in which they are usually thought, in their native tongue, so to speak. I always speak French when I wish to discuss life as it is really lived. Tell me, how are you feeling now? Do you have vertigo, for example?"

Bogges did feel off-balance, as though he or the chair he was sitting in was floating at a sharp angle a foot off the carpet. "No," lied Bogges.

"Vertigo," continued Dr. Fall smoothly, "is or can be a psychological condition manifested as a disturbance of the sensible equipment. But where does that disturbance originate, Mr. Bogges? Nowadays, we would say from a neurosis, a psychological trauma. It might interest you to note that once vertigo was associated with the Devil. Of course, we no longer believe in the Devil but, nevertheless, He had His uses. At least you knew what you were dealing with. That should appeal to you. One might say that His masterpiece, the great work of the master of illusion, is His present success in passing Himself off as nonexistent. He has every interest in doing so."

For a moment, Dr. Fall flickered out of sight. Bogges blinked, and the psychiatrist came back into focus, somewhat larger and for some reason rather goatish. Bogges thought he detected an odor of burning hair.

Dr. Fall waved an arm, which seemed to extend itself unnaturally, and the odor dispersed. "Spirit and free will, since you object to French, those are also unfashionable. They disappeared with the Devil, not by accident. You can't have one without the other. What would be the use?"

Again, Bogges felt himself lifted into the air. The chair tilted to the left, gave a little shake and, as though exhausted, fell with two bumps. Bogges experienced a profound lethargy. His tongue lay paralyzed.

"No, there's no response, Mr. Bogges. It is true that free will, the spirit, is a sanctuary, but only when you act is it inaccessible. That is why indolence is so dangerous. Nevertheless, the Old Gentleman does not directly affect the spiritual faculties, only indirectly, by disturbing from outside the sensible equipment, your body," the voice grew in volume. It seemed to roar. "The senses," said the roar, "material objects." Then the volume was abruptly turned down, like a radio, "and so on," said the now barely audible voice.

The time had come to act. Bogges rocked his haunches back and forth in order to build up the necessary momentum to pitch himself out of the recliner. When a sufficiently acute angle was achieved, he tensed his thighs and rose to the upright. He went 'round the desk and grasped Dr. Fall's goatee in both hands. He pulled, and the face came away with the beard. The remaining blankness had an inquiring expression. Bogges had questions of his own. Then he woke in his green rocking club chair in the front parlor. This is what came of reading Father Joseph de Tonquedec, SJ. What had possessed him to read such infernal nonsense? He sat thinking over his dream. He grew comfortable; a voluptuous indolence came over him. He cast about for an activity which might count as an exercise of the will, to prevent further demonic assault according to Dr. Fall's analysis yet still allow him to remain sitting. The thought came to him that perhaps it might actually be a good idea to contribute a letter to the paper. Framing a letter, or finding a subject for a letter, or at least choosing a pseudonym for the correspondent should count as exercising the will. After a while, the name Chakravarti occurred to him; S. J. Chakravarti would do nicely, taking revenge in a mild way on the Jesuit priest who had conjured up the Devil and exorcised sleep. Bogges was confident that now that he had a name, a subject would sooner or later present itself. Meanwhile, it was time for bed.

The next morning, Bogges got himself up, bathed, dressed, breakfasted, and out the door with no more than the customary difficulties. Progress to the bus stop on M Street was satisfactory. He encountered no dogs of any kind. The bus arrived promptly; there was a vacant seat near the front. He sat down next to a hard-faced woman in a halter top and jeans that didn't quite cover her navel. Her hair had been made up into innumerable pig or rat tails. Bogges looked away. Above, a poster exhorted him to consider that if he were not part of the solution, he must be part of the problem, solution and problem both unspecified.

He got off near the office, in front of Marina's Italian Restaurant. Jesus, the Guatemalan busboy, was sweeping the sidewalk. His face had a look of the utmost seriousness, squat features and eyes like clay dinner plates were a model for a totem. To aid concentration, Jesus was making gargling and clicking noises from somewhere in his throat. While he'd been walking north to the border, he'd fallen in with a patrol of Mexican soldiers. They'd kept him company for a few days, and Jesus had been glad of their companionship. When their ways parted, the soldiers had robbed him. Jesus had been grateful they'd left him his clothing and his sandals. But then the soldiers had fought over the contents of his purse, and one had been killed. At first the soldiers were going to kill Jesus too, but in the end they took pity on him and only cut out his tongue.

"Hello, Jesus," said Bogges.

Jesus stopped sweeping and rested on his broom. He gargled and clicked solemnly, nodded his head once, and went back to work. Bogges admired Jesus's concentration on the task at hand, and then for some reason he thought again about that puzzling exhortation from the poster on the bus: If you're not part of the solution, you're part of the problem. What could this have to do with Jesus, or Bogges for that matter? It was the dictum of a professional busybody, a kind of terrorist, he at once decided. People really should just mind their own business he told himself. Bogges watched Jesus for a moment more, then hurried off to work, a stout, preoccupied figure pitching and listing on stubby pins, eager to assume the voice of that worthy oriental gentlemen S. J. Chakravarti and put his thoughts on paper.

CHAPTER TWO

Sir, as life long citizen for twenty years just now, I am telling you with too much sorrow that people are not minding their business. Drivers are not knowing my destination. Bankers are not knowing my check. Supermarkets are not selling food of first freshness and tastiness. Waiters are telling me their names and I am not wanting to know. Strangers are ringing up on telephone and calling me S.J. I am telling all strangers, to you I am not S.J., I am Mr. Chakravarti!

Why is this, I am asking? I am answering: people are not minding their business. People are saying how I am not thinking how women are thinking, or people not speaking English or people not sleeping with opposite sex or so very many things I am not wanting to think about. I am saying nothing and they are saying I am making statement. In this country not making statement is statement and I am wondering what is remaining when people are not keeping quiet when they are not talking. When I am not talking I am saying nothing and when I am not thinking I am not having thoughts. As American citizen this is my right. So, I am saying: whatever you are wanting I am not giving. Also, I am saying to fellow citizens please to shut up and mind your own business.

Respectfully,
S.J. Chakravarti

Bogges pulled the sheet from his typewriter, the last to remain at the paper. The Hermes 3000 reminded him of a '55 Chevy, gracefully squat, streamlined and bulky at the same time, much like himself. Its pale green enamel was soothing. Its mechanical pounding helped concentrate the mind. He'd had to fight to keep it when the computer people had come to wire the office. He'd taken to locking his door at night so that no one could steal his machine away in the dark. The cleaning staff didn't mind: one less office to look after. Bogges took the trash out every evening.

He was pleased with his morning's work. The tone was right, the sentiments unimpeachable. He thought he'd enjoy Chakravarti's prose one more time before turning to the pile of readers' letters on his desk. He was just getting to these, the customary mix—belaboring the obvious, crankish hobby-horses, illiterate laments, obscene threats—when a voice at the door interrupted him.

"What ho, Eustace. Tell me what's it all about. What's new, what's happening, what's, er, what?"

Lance Morrow-Graves, to whom the voice belonged, was Bogges's boss, the assistant managing editor in charge of odds and ends, Letters, Religion, Science, Obituaries, the sections the executive editor and the publisher didn't care about. Morrow-Graves always spoke this way. He was Canadian and secretly felt that he was an imitation American. Bogges thought he had got that part right. The imitation Englishman, however, did not come off so successfully.

"Are you busy, Eustace?" came the voice again.

"Mind your own business," said Bogges sharply.

"I say, I was only asking if I might come in. If it's inconvenient, I'll come back later."

Bogges decided he'd gone too far. "Come in, Lance. That wasn't directed at you. I was thinking about the letter I was just reading. The writer seems to think the world would be a better place if people would simply mind their own business. He makes some interesting points. It's not the sort of letter we usually get. Here, take a seat over there."

Bogges gestured toward a stack of books and journals on a hard wooden chair set too close to the floor for Morrow-Graves's six feet plus. Morrow-Graves eyed the proffered seat with ambivalence, decided against. He pushed his back into the door frame. Now that he'd been given permission to enter, he had apparently changed his mind. He put his thumbs into the little front slits of his tweed vest and looked up at the ceiling as though searching for something.

"What do you know about God, Eustace?"

Bogges involuntarily looked up at the ceiling. "He's not there."

Morrow-Graves tore his gaze away from the ceiling and looked down at Bogges. He made a fizzing noise. "Oh, very good, very good indeed. I was looking at the ceiling and I asked you what you know about God and you said he's not there, meaning not that he's not there at all but that he's not there on the ceiling." Morrow-Graves smiled indulgently. "Seriously now," he said, "what do you know about the Old Fellow. Answer carefully. There's a reason for this, ah, interrogation."

"I know that if God is omnipotent, he does not need to exist to save us."

"No, I suppose not. But, of course, we know that He exists. Didn't someone say that if you can imagine Him, He exists?"

"Up to a point," said Bogges.

Morrow-Graves was evidently thinking about Anselm and the ontological proof. Bogges wondered if he should clarify the matter for him, enlighten his ignorance, beat him over the head with his superior learning. He thought he might.

"Anselm," said Bogges, "who lived into the early twelfth century, said that God was the being than whom none greater can exist. But if the being than whom none greater can exist existed only in the intellect, he would not be the greatest, because you could add reality to the conception. Anselm argued that it followed from this that God necessarily had, or has, real existence."

"Yes, that's just what I was saying." Morrow-Graves looked pleased with himself. "Eustace, I've noticed that you have grown a little stale of late. The letters page is not as lively as it's been in the past."

"Our readers are not as lively, or maybe the lively ones don't write letters anymore," said Bogges.

"No, no, Eustace, you see, you are tired. The readers who write us are the committed ones, the most engaged. It follows that they are lively. I want a page that reflects that."

"Short of supplying the letters myself, I don't see how you can obtain a livelier page. Anyway, it doesn't necessarily follow that those readers are lively, if by lively you mean bright, thoughtful, full of spirit. By and large they have an ax to grind and the energy to lick an envelope and affix a stamp."

Morrow-Graves looked troubled. "No, no, of course we can't have you writing the letters, it would ruin the whole point of the page." He walked over to the pile of letters on Bogges's desk and idly read the one from the top.

"Now consider this one, Eustace, this Chakravarti fellow, his English is deplorable, of course, you'll have to clean it up for him, but he makes some good points. Why, just the other day, at my bank, I had to show eight pieces of identification before I could cash a check. I'd dealt with the teller for years, too. But it was as if I had walked in for the first time. Now here's a letter worth publishing, and here it is sitting on your desk."

"It just came in this morning."

"Eustace, Eustace, the mail is delivered at two o'clock. Admit it, you've had enough of letters. You want something new." Again Morrow-Graves smiled indulgently.

Bogges searched for a way out of the trap he'd set for himself. "This was delivered by messenger," he said quickly. "See, there's no envelope."

"Let's not quibble, Eustace, especially since I have a plum assignment for you. I want you to edit Religion for me."

You mean elaborate, said Bogges, wiseacreing to himself. Out loud, he said, "I don't know anything about religion."

"Of course you do. Why, you know all about this, er, Anselm character from, when was it, the Crusades."

Bogges cursed himself for showing off. A miniature black poodle suddenly appeared perched on Morrow-Graves's shoulder. The dog extended a pink tongue and licked Morrow-Graves's ear. The hallucination vanished, and Bogges's pulse raced. His face became purple.

"Are you alright, Eustace?"

"This has come as a shock, Lance. I'm happy here at Letters."

Morrow-Graves smiled an understanding smile while maintaining a look of concern. The effect was lugubrious. "Life is movement," he pronounced. "Yes, life is movement. So it follows, doesn't it, that the more you move, the more you live?"

"Yes, Lance, that follows."

Morrow-Graves was encouraged. "Eustace, it will do you and the section a power of good to make this move. It's a good idea. You do believe in the power of good ideas, don't you?"

"No more than I do in the other kind." This slipped out before Bogges could stop it.

Morrow-Graves's llama-like face lit up. "Ha, ha, you've made another joke. I asked if you believed in the power of good ideas, and you said no more than in the other kind, meaning bad ideas. But seriously, I suppose bad ideas have power too. Why, look at Communism. That was a bad idea, wasn't it?"

"Yes, Lance, it was."

"Although," Morrow-Graves said thoughtfully, "the Chinese seem fond of it."

"Probably only the ones who are running things," said Bogges.

"Hmm, I see what you mean. Not as much fun for those who have to take orders. Still, someone has to give orders."

"Why?"

"Why? Because, well, where would we be?"

"I'd still be editing Letters, for one."

"But you are editing Letters."

Bogges was about to remind him bitterly that Letters had just been taken away from him. Then he recollected that it was a characteristic of Morrow-Graves to lose track, that one idea always supplanted another to the point where the first ceased to exist. Madmen, so Bogges had read, were noted for their ability to hold two opposing ideas in their heads at the same time. Morrow-Graves, by this definition, must be eminently sane; the opportunity would be seized.

"As you say," said Bogges, his turn to smile benignly, "I am the Letters editor. In fact, I have a stack of them to get through. You don't mind, do you?"

"No, of course not. Far be it from me to interfere with a man's job. Keep up the good work. We'll talk again later." Morrow-Graves put his thumbs back into his vest and, humming to himself, left with head bent as if deep in thought.

When Bogges was alone, he attacked the pile of unread letters. His reading held no surprises. There were numerous irritable complaints from residents of the better sections of Washington: dead trees, unfilled potholes, uncollected garbage, unsolved crimes, insolent, unresponsive police, traffic wardens, firemen, licensing clerks, sundry city employees. It was the paper's policy never to print these letters, under the principle that conditions were worse in the largely Black sections of town. That those citizens seldom wrote in complaint reinforced management's conviction that the policy was sound: benign neglect and equal treatment, the best of both worlds.

A letter from the Nigerian ambassador would see print. He complained that a recent news story about corruption in Lagos was racist. "Our form of government follows a different cultural model," wrote His Excellency. Also to be published was an indignant note from the chargé d'affaires at the French Embassy. He denied that the routine arrest of gypsies in Paris was prompted by racial stereotyping. "After all," he protested, "they commit most of the crimes."

Bogges mechanically excised the Nigerian's paen to the current president-for-life and an analysis of the Napoleonic Code from the Frenchman. He eyed the letters remaining to be read with distaste, sighed, and went back to work. He had disposed of most of these by noon, had found three others he could run, not on racial subjects, and, having filled his page, took his work, including Chakravarti's letter, down the hall to the copy editor. Robinson, whether this was his first name, his last name, his only name, an alias, was one of the paper's mysteries. He was an old hippie radical, ill-mannered and pointedly unkempt. But he approved of Bogges's refusal to give up his typewritter— "got to fuck with the System, Man"—and would scan Bogges's edited letters into the layout program as though the revolution depended on it. Robinson also helped Bogges cover his tracks by erasing letters emailed to the paper as they arrived. No one had noticed how few letters came to the paper as a result of this practice likely because no one cared about readers' letters. Duty done, Bogges left for lunch.

While he stood at the restaurant bar waiting for his dozen Belons and carafe of white he eyed the crowd, hoping no one he knew would be there to interrupt his meal by talking to him. It seemed that the coast was clear. He tackled the wine and shellfish, when they came, with some degree of security. Bogges liked to think about what he was eating when he was eating. This was minding the business at hand. The brininess of the oysters and the odor of ocean that rose from their fluid married nicely to the tang of the white. The carafe was barely below the halfway mark when he squeezed lemon over the last oyster. It was a rule that these things must come out even. Bogges weighed the relative merits of another dozen, which might entail ordering more wine, or a half dozen, which would require an increase in drinking velocity. He had settled on the half dozen when a hand gripped his drinking arm. The hand belonged to Jonah Thomas, a fellow editor, an eager and earnest young man in charge of Life and Styles. He liked to be called JT. Bogges had made it a point never to do this even before the younger man had involved himself with Sally Benton, Bogges's former wife.

"Let go of my arm," said Bogges.

"Come off it. You can drink with the other, can't you?"

"What business is it of yours?"

"Take the arm. I don't want it. I was just being friendly."

This was a lie. While regaining possession of his arm, Bogges managed to jab his elbow into Thomas's waist. Thomas winced.

"There's no cause to get belligerent. I've got good news for you. Sally and I are getting married. You won't have to pay alimony anymore. That should make you happy. You don't like spending money on other people, right? It's the Scot in you, isn't it?"

"Irish," said Bogges. "I'm of Irish descent. Not that it matters."

"Ulster," said Thomas. "It's the Calvinist strain. I can spot it every time."

Having scored this point, Thomas smirked. This made his regular features look even more childish. Bogges thought he'd retaliate. He assumed his Samuel Johnson voice. The sound of his merriment, he said to himself in anticipation, is like the call of trumpets and the beating of drums, to drown out the cries of the wounded and the dying.

"How good of God," said Bogges sententiously, "to arrange this marriage."

He waited to deliver the punch line so that Thomas would be truly caught off guard. When the smirk began to metamorphose into something resembling a smile, Bogges resumed. "Yes, how good of God to arrange things so that two people should be miserable instead of four."

Thomas's expression hardened. "What did Sally ever see in you?"

"I expect she wanted to experience a real man; of course, it was too much for her. It must have been a great relief to have stumbled across you."

Thomas stiffened. His shoulders hunched. A hand clenched. Bogges, who felt that his bulk served equally to enlarge or oppress a company, hoped that Thomas would strike out. He waited inside his substantial mass. Thomas seemed undecided. While he was thinking about his next move, Bogges filled his glass and drank. He gave a sigh of satisfaction, which Thomas echoed by an exhalation of breath. When Bogges looked at Thomas again, Thomas had mastered whatever impulses he had to over-come.

"Tell me," said Thomas with feigned interest, "what does it feel like to be an asshole without a friend in the world?"

Bogges was benign. He patted his belly, turned his hippo countenance on Thomas. "I lead a rich interior life."

"Only you would think that your miles of gut are a substitute for living."

"You're wrong, Thomas. My bellyful of gut is merely the outward sign of lengthy ruminations. If you could read my entrails, you would follow the twists and turns of the human soul. My gut, my capacious gut, my Gargantuan gut, so big and yet so small, so digressive and yet so compact, this gut of mine finds a place for everything in the sublunary sphere and beyond the golden sun. Animal, vegetable and mineral, I have swallowed the world and, thanks to this great gut, I have digested. Inside the workings of my gut are to be found war and peace, crime and punishment, sense and sensibility. My honest gut tells me what has been, what is, what will be. I look out from the fortress of my gut and I see across all the vastness of space and time. My thirsting, hungering, insatiable gut is the microcosm where all things come to be, perish, are reborn. The miracle of my gut is a living picture of apprehension, an image of creation. It receives the staff of life midway through its journey of nourishment and makes it my own. You chew, you swallow, you're done with it. Your pathetic form takes over unconsciously. But I, in this magnificent body, follow every movement, every secretion. When food and drink first pass my lips, it is as though I read a passage from the Great Author. I swallow, and the belly acids begin their work of digestion; it is like the breaking down of a thought into its constituent parts. Already I have the pleasant sense that meaning, in the form of protein, vitamins, and minerals no less than in subject and object, has come to fill my being. But this is only the beginning; the belly is the superficial organ. Genesis, true absorption occurs in the intestine, the sacred gut. This gut of meaning contracts and propels onward. It squeezes necessity from the crude stuff of experience. The intestinal secretions, with the aid of forthright bile and subtle pancreatic juices flowing through innumerable projections, alter the food into useful elements for proper distribution by blood and lymph. Is this not like the imagination? Just so, when I reflect, consider, ponder the innumerable sensations of existence, I grasp some new notion and place it in my memory like a new layer of muscle, new cells which, in their turn, will reach out and grasp and combine. My gut grows like the mind learning. The mind seizes on the phenomenal and abstracts the spiritual. My gut grasps the material and extracts the essential. My gut is the logos."

"My God," said Thomas, "you're drunk."

"There is a god in the grape," replied Bogges with composure. "And the grape is in my gut."

"Your gut is your god, God help you."

"Yes, He does. The God in my gut is my shepherd. He shall not want. I feed him and He speaks." Bogges swallowed air. "I am inspired," he announced with a burp. "The God in my gut, who is a Spirit, comes numinously forth. From liquids and solids comes the Divine Gas."

"You should go see someone," said Thomas.

"The weakness of your retorts reflect the poverty of your being."

Thomas knew the world envied him, and he liked to think he carried this burden with grace. He arched his back and made prominent his flat belly. "I've got energy and drive. I'll be the executive editor one day. You heard it here."

"Yes, having no talent is not enough anymore," said Bogges, stealing the line from someone he couldn't immediately place. "It takes much more than an absence of imagination to succeed these days."

"That's rich, coming from you, belly worshipper. I hear Lance is moving you to Religion."

It didn't occur to Bogges to wonder how Thomas knew. It was Thomas's business, it was his being, to know such things before anyone else. Mechanically, Bogges denied he was being moved.

"Lance changed his mind," he said.

"Well, when the breeze blows from another quarter he'll change it back again. Next it will be Obits. That fits even better. You're a dead man, Eustace, and you don't even know it. If you're still around when I'm running things, I'll fire you personally."

"I look forward to your continuing elevation."

"You just don't get it, do you? I'm on the way up. You're on the way down. I guess you haven't heard they've given me Sunday Books and The Magazine. You were interested in Books, weren't you?"

Bogges was shaken. The fact was, he had been interested in editing Books, although there was very little being written nowadays he liked. On the whole, Bogges thought that rather qualified him for the post. He could see that he'd been bested. As one who seldom read anything but his reporters' copy, who preferred computers to books, who fundamentally didn't like books at all, Thomas had superior qualifications.

"Who'll be doing Life And Styles?" asked Bogges despite himself.

Thomas grinned. "Oh, I still have that. Yes, it's quite a nice little empire I'm carving out for myself." Thomas wasn't quite finished with him. "Now that Sally's got her MA in communications, thanks to your checks, I'm going to give her a column, 'Benton on Books,' or maybe 'Bent on Books.' I'm sure you'll enjoy reading her, seeing what we got for your money. So long, Eustace. See you around."

He swaggered out with the lithe gait of one who religiously exercises. The wine seemed to have mysteriously soured. Bogges finished it anyway and went off to Marina's Italian Restaurant for an extensive feed. It wasn't true that Bogges had no friends. They just weren't the sort of people Thomas would bother with. They weren't useful people, not if you were interested in getting ahead. They were merely people Bogges liked to talk to, even listen to. Marina listened as well as she talked; her cooking was superb.

Fasting is a cause of melancholy recited Bogges to himself as he settled comfortably into Marina's private booth next to the kitchen. The little restaurant was dark and crowded with diners attentive to what they found on their plates. The sound of their voices, the clatter and clink of glasses and cutlery, was soothing, subdued and muffled by the surroundings, the uncompromisingly dated wallpaper, a green flocked felt depicting Italian vistas, the thick Chianti-colored carpet and the damask tablecloths.

The room smelled of basil and sage, olive oil and sharp cheese. Through a swinging glass door Bogges could watch Marina among her pots. Her heavily browed face and bright eyes set somewhat too close to the bridge of her nose made one think of a monkey, but an attractive monkey. The French phrase suddenly, nightmarishly, occurred to Bogges: beauté de singe. Well, it was a sort of monkey beauty, but beauty nonetheless. Marina's blueish-white skin was very fine, and so was her slender figure. As she moved about her work she gave no impression of haste or bustle. Her movements were meticulous and graceful. Jesus appeared with bread and wine. He went back through the glass door, and Bogges saw him put his hand on Marina's arm. When he had her attention, he pointed to where Bogges was sitting. Marina waved, ladled soup into a tureen, and sent it out with Jesus. The soup was followed by tiny meatballs and capellini in a thin sauce where the flavor of port dominated, then a magnificently oily scallopini of veal, salty with prosciutto and aromatic with sage. Later, Marina herself came out with two glasses of grappa.

"I can only sit a minute," she said in her sweet, breathy voice. "Chin-chin."

"Cheers."

Marina threw back her drink. Bogges sipped.

"What kind of a drink was that?" asked Marina with simulated indignation.

"You gave me three times what you had in your glass."

"Well, you are three times my size."

"Surely only two times."

"How much do you weigh?" she asked.

"You tell me first," said Bogges.

"A lady does not reveal such things."

"I know how much you weigh."

"Oh? How do you know that?"

"I know you weigh no more than you need to and your weight is just the right amount for your size and your size is just right for your shape and your shape suits you."

Marina looked pleased. "My cooking has made you gallant."

"And your company."

Marina looked even more pleased. "You are almost handsome when you pay me such compliments, like a great kindly beast."

Bogges laughed.

"What's funny?" she asked.

Bogges was about to tell Marina his thoughts on her animal beauty. He decided not to. "Not everyone thinks I'm kind."

"I'm sure you're only cruel to people who deserve it. Some people must be treated harshly, no? So they won't oppress you."

"I think that sums it up."

"I am going to close the restaurant on Sundays."

"Good. You work too hard."

"I am going to do some living. I have two tickets to the symphony, a wonderful flute player will play a concerto. I love the flute, better than the violin. It has the voice the angels use to speak."

Bogges thought this was dubious. Angels sang, so far as he knew, and probably used their voices to do it. On the other hand, they probably didn't have voice boxes, or throats, or lungs, or diaphragms since, being spirits, they didn't have bodies. So perhaps they did use flutes, although how they managed to play them without lips wasn't clear.

Marina was beaming. "I have been considering which of my gentlemen friends to invite. I think I will invite you."

"I accept only on condition that you'll allow me to take you to dinner afterwards."

They agreed to meet on Sunday at the Kennedy Center, and Marina went back to the kitchen. Bogges experienced a pleasant sense of repletion on the short walk back to the paper, the savor of which was heightened in the elevator ride up to his floor by a prolonged eructation. The afternoon mail had arrived to clutter his desk. He pushed it aside and put his feet up. Soon he was asleep.

CHAPTER THREE

The grappa was at war with the oysters. When Dr. Fall materialized, wearing a suit and matching cap in checkered brown and yellow, he seemed to be an image of Bogges's indigestion. He sat himself down on the chair of books Morrow-Graves had rejected and examined his bare wrist like a child playing at having a watch.

"It's time we began, Mr. Bogges."

Dr. Fall glanced again at his wrist and tapped it. The puerile attempt to create the illusion he was telling time charged the gesture with malevolence. Bogges experienced a more violent churning in his gut.

"Many of my patients suffer intestinal discomfort during our sessions. This is normal. Indeed, the discomfort can even be put to good use. It should suggest to you the absurdity of the mind-body dichotomy."

"Got you," said Bogges, gleeful despite his stomachache, "you are going to rehash what I told Thomas and pretend it's yours."

"And what does that mean to you?"

"Oh, no you don't. You're not going to entangle me in your nonsense."

Dr. Fall was indulgent. "I think this is worth exploring together. Your mind and body are merely different forms of the same organ. I believe you already hold this view. Your mind apprehends that you will be facing some unpleasant truths. Your body articulates, as best it can, this fact, thus your indigestion. My patients come to me so that they can see clearly what torments them. Therapy is difficult, even hellish, Mr. Bogges, and Hell, if you will permit the fancy, is the unpleasant truth. Once we've got at that, really gotten to the bottom of things, well, I won't say your anguish will be over, but your doubts will be. Now, it's time we began."

Dr. Fall tapped his wrist again, and this time it seemed contemptible, merely a piece of incompetent playacting, a third-rate pose.

"What a terrible phony you are," said Bogges.

"It is customary," said Dr. Fall, "to resist the therapist in the beginning. You will get over this phase because you want to. Otherwise, why would you be here?"

"You're the one who's not here. You are less than an imposter. You're a bogus bogey, an afternoon nap's nightmare. You don't exist at all, except in my imagination."

"I don't think you are yet competent to distinguish between the imaginary and the real, Mr. Bogges. It is a characteristic symptom of your condition."

"What is my condition?"

"Mortality, Mr. Bogges. But come, we're wasting time. Let us begin, once and for all."

"I suppose you're going to twist things I already know, the way dreams twist everything so that it seems new. You can't know anything I don't because you are only my dream."

"Dreams are a form of consciousness, Mr. Bogges. Let us not argue. We will agree that I am a dream. Still, you are conscious of me. I am satisfied with that. As for my telling you things you already know, we won't argue about that either. After all, you do not know what you know. I might add that confusion or bewilderment about such things is a further characteristic of your condition."

"When I hear you talk, I know that I know nothing. You are nothing."

"You are playing with words again. Something of a vieux jeu, I must say."

Bogges twitched at the French.

"My apologies. I had forgotten your antipathy to that useful tongue. Would you prefer that I spoke German? It used to be my favorite language."

"No. Yes. Speak in German. I don't know it. You can't know it either."

"Ich bin ein Berliner."

"What nonsense. Everyone knows Kennedy said that. Is that the best you can do?"

"ARBEIT MACHT FREI"

"Yes, over the gates of Auschwitz, that's the other piece of German I know. Your unreality is the most vivid thing about you."

Bogges suddenly felt his intestines knot. A mailed fist or animal paw went clawing out of them, and up his stomach to his throat.

Dr. Fall smiled. "I am also a Parisian, a Muscovite, a Londoner, a Washingtonian. I am a citizen of the world, in short, a cosmopolitan, at home everywhere and never at home." Dr. Fall twinkled at Bogges. "But we are not here to talk about me. How is your stomach? If you are more comfortable now, perhaps we can begin."

Bogges felt well enough, barely, to repeat, "Begin?"

"Yes, at the beginning," said Dr. Fall, "the very beginning. Let us begin with the dawn of consciousness. You do not remember your mother giving you suck, I suppose?"

"Of course not. Anyway, what difference would that make?"

"Beginnings are always important. What comes after follows what came before, follows it according to law. Perhaps we will find time to work out those laws as they apply to you. Let us hope so. Suffice it to say, there are laws, and that is why the present comes out of the past, the future from the present."

"You are talking nonsense again," said Bogges. "Don't bore me with your tautologies."

"If you knew, Mr. Bogges, knew for a fact and in detail how consciousness first came to man, do you not think that might explain a good deal?"

"You are now going to tell me the story of Adam and Eve? Don't waste your breath, Doctor, if you are a doctor. The story is familiar to me; otherwise you wouldn't be able to tell it to me."

"The story is only familiar to you in outline."

"You don't mean you know the details."

"I will let you be the judge. Naturally, the version you know is an allegory. Paradise, for example, what the real paradise was like, well, I'll let you be the judge of that too."

Dr. Fall crossed his legs under himself and extended his arms palms up like a storyteller from *The Arabian Nights*. Except that in his checked suit and cap he looked more like a racing tout. He began.

"Towards the end of the Pleistocene, on the fifth of May, to be exact, one million four thousand and fifteen years ago—that is, once upon a time—a female anthropoid ape awoke at dawn. Unconsciously, because hitherto her life, like that of her troop, had been an existence of undifferentiated sensation, she scratched her armpits and breakfasted off the lice she had dislodged. When she was finished eating, she looked down from the tree she had climbed into for safety the night before. The edge of the forest, a few yards off, gave way to savannah, a treeless plain, boggy in the rainy season. The animal, why don't we call her Eve, had fastened her gaze on a watering hole less turbid than most and within easy jumping distance of a tree limb which extended out over the plain. A red sun rose and innumerable patches of water turned molten. The primaeval landscape was dotted with an undulating fire. A faint breath of wind before true day's heat stirred the grasses. Eve was startled. She chattered indignantly. Then movement subsided and Eve fell silent. When she felt secure, she swung down from her tree and drew herself as erect as her curved spine allowed. She approached the watering hole. She sniffed. Ah, the fecund scents of the Pleistocene, mossy so that algae might grow in the nostrils, teeming with the fecal odor of thriving bacteria. She stooped, drank. Some hours before, a cloudburst had swelled a rivulet. This rivulet disappeared into a limestone shelf which, through a course of underground channels, sprang up under Eve's watering hole. As a result, the pool had been freshened that morning and was, briefly, that very moment, perfectly clear. Eve continued her drink. The sun rose higher. The pool turned to silver. Eve lifted her dripping muzzle from the water to breathe. She caught sight of her reflection. This was the first time she had seen herself, although she did not yet know it was she. She clawed in defensive fright at the water, and the apparition disappeared in the turbulence. Warily she waited to see if it was safe to satisfy her thirst. Soon her tongue was lapping at the water. Again, her reflection took shape before her. She jumped back and up, gripping the tree limb behind her in one muscular prehensile paw. Why did she not swing deeper into the forest, into the safety of the dense foliage? Why, Mr. Bogges, did she hang there suspended from a branch, glaring at the pool? Because she was thirsty. The breakfast lice were unusually salty! It was a few milligrams of excess salt and a cloudburst that brought the human race to consciousness. Thirst and a mirror, Mr. Bogges, they explain everything. So Eve swung there, chattering with rage. She shook her free paw at the apparition in the watering hole. She glared. She looked in vain for something to throw at the enemy in the water. When she looked back at the watering hole, it was deserted. She dropped down from the limb and advanced cautiously. She peered over the edge. Startled eyes set close to the bridge of a broad and hairy nose stared back. Eve withdrew her face, and the reflection disappeared. Why did she not strike out this time? The cranial capacity of the animal, six hundred and forty cubic centimeters, was just great enough, and the brain inside just complex enough, for Eve to have the first thought. Spurred by her own reflection, Eve became aware that something was looking out from inside her skull. She moaned and gibbered, and the sound of her own voice terrified her. She had heard her sounds and noises all her life, but she had heard them uncomprehendingly, as part of the general background of a being for which there was no foreground. Suddenly there was, dimly, a she to hear. This was terror of a new kind: What made that noise? What is inside looking out? What is it looking out from? Thus was Eve exiled from Paradise, Mr. Bogges. Subject and object came into being that day. The universe shivered, and was split asunder. Eve quivered with rage. She wished to strike out. The enemy was there, hiding in the pool. Had she not seen it disappear into the water?

She bared her fangs and launched herself. For one brief instant, she saw the hated object rushing at her. The battle was over the moment it was met. A boulder lay just below the surface. Eve struck head-foremost. The impact split her skull in two.

"The other members of her troop had watched the epiphany of self-consciousness from a safe distance. When it became apparent that no animal was near to eat the corpse, they emerged from the forest and pulled Eve's body from the pool, now reddened by her blood. They dragged her back to the forest and consumed her remains.

"For some three thousand generations, Eve's descendants continued to exist in the Paradise of undifferentiated sensation. It was a momentary reprieve. There came a time forty thousand years after when two male Australopithecines fighting over a mate caused the female, Eve's true daughter, to once again emerge into self-consciousness. The survivor of that combat chased down Eve's daughter and, during the rape, became Adam."

"What did he do then?" said Bogges in a strangled voice. "After he became Adam, I mean."

Dr. Fall smiled briefly. "He struck her, naturally."

Bogges thought he had known the story of Adam and Eve the way he knew many things, odds and ends of the mind like items of old clothing: not to be discarded, not to be worn. He was surprised to feel grief.

"You are a bastard," said Bogges.

"No names, please, Mr. Bogges. I do not allow name-calling. I find it counterproductive."

Bogges went over the story he'd been taught. There didn't seem to be much resemblance to the repugnant horror Dr. Fall had retailed. Dr. Fall seemed to read his mind.

"Perhaps I do know things you do not. Of course, dreams are prescient. Why shouldn't they be able to predict the unknown past as well as the unknown future?"

"One doesn't predict the past," said Bogges.

"There, you are wrong. Economists and Wall Street analysts do it for a living."

"They do it to guess the future."

"Yes, that is where we began. You must know what came before to understand why you are here and where, perhaps, it is to be hoped, you will end up."

"In the long run, we're all dead," said Bogges, predicting the future.

"You quote an economist, good. It's one of my best subjects. Although you hardly need be an economist to hold that very little of significance occurred between the dawn of consciousness and the invention of credit. I might go further and argue that the invention of money was humanity's second truly creative act: after all, how often is something created out of nothing?"

Bogges stirred. His feet slipped from the desk. He awoke with a start. Dr. Fall was gone. Bogges's one friend at the paper, Abel Japrowski, editor of Business and Finance, was staring at him from the door with a smile.

"Sorry to interrupt your nap, Eustace. Was it a long night or a long lunch?"

"Both," said Bogges groggily, then, "I need to pee."

"I'll go to the men's with you."

"Right."

Bogges heaved himself stiffly out of his chair. He felt shaken. He put a hand on the desk to steady himself. The mail rustled. He watched dismayed the pile of letters rise and float nonchalantly in the air. As though bored with this parlor trick, the envelopes snapped impatiently against each other, like a card-sharp riffling through the deck. Then, from sheer indolence, the letters fell and scattered on the floor.

"Did you see that?" asked Bogges.

"What, you knocking over the mail?"

"I didn't touch it."

"Come on, Eustace, you're not awake."

"Maybe."

The two men walked in silence down the corridor. Japrowski was no taller than Bogges, but he was a hundred pounds lighter. He adjusted his pace to match his companion's. In the men's room, they faced the urinals and contemplated the plumbing.

"I've been having a recurring dream," said Bogges when they were zip-
ping up.

"What's she like?"

"No, not a girl."

"A boy?"

"No, Abel."

"Well, what's the problem?"

"I've been dreaming about a psychiatrist. At least, that's what he calls
himself."

"They are notorious liars. You're right to be suspicious."

'Yes, that's it. I think he's a terrible liar."

Japrowski's saturnine and speculative countenance brightened with interest. "Do you think he's lying to you in the dream or after you wake up?"

"Both."

"Unusual."

"What do you mean?"

"I mean, by the way, if we're done here, we could go back to your office."

They returned to Bogges's small space.

"It's not customary to think you're being lied to while you're dreaming,"
continued Japrowski. "After you wake up, that's a different matter."

"That's the odd thing. He's so vivid, I think I'm actually arguing with
him."

"What does he call himself?"

"Dr. Grippin Fall."

"You're kidding."

"He's a very crappy character."

"He sounds like a phony to me."

"That's what I told him."

"What did he say?"

"He said that he didn't mind what I thought about him, so long as I was
conscious of him."

"What did you say?"

"I can't remember. Oh, yes, he started telling me the story of Adam and
Eve."

"Why did he do that?"

"Why do you keep referring to him as though he were real?"

"Fine. Why did you dream that this Dr. Fall character told you the story of Adam and Eve?"

"I don't know. That's why I'm going over this with you. His story wasn't anything like the real story. I mean, the story in the Bible."

"What was it like?"

"It wasn't like a story at all, more like a documentary."

"Oh, in what way?"

"It was all facts, unpleasant, distasteful facts, the kind someone would choose if they were going out of their way to be rude."

"It sounds more like a newspaper," said Japrowski. "What actually did he tell you?"

"That Eve was an ape-man, or ape-woman I suppose, millions of years ago in the forest. She was the first animal to become conscious of herself as a self, and that is what the exile from Paradise really means. Then forty thousand years later, another ape-woman became conscious of herself and when she was raped by an ape-man he became Adam. But the way he told the story, with colors and smells and sounds, made it seem that he knew what he was talking about, as if he had been there, witnessed these events. The last thing he said, just before you woke me up, was that the only important thing that happened in human history after that was the invention of money."

"And you really don't know why you had this dream?"

"I'm not sure."

"I think it's fairly obvious," said Japrowski with a smile. "Morrow-Graves wants to transfer you to Religion."

"Does everyone know about this?".

"Yes. Anyway, I imagine you don't much want to leave Letters."

"God, no."

"So you had a troubling dream prompted by the, ah, prospect of the new job. You sensed that I was in your office before you were fully awake, and so the last thing you dreamt about was money."

Bogges was annoyed with his friend. His explanation had the lifeless plausibility that made common sense so dispiriting.

"Well, I don't think that's what happened at all," said Bogges rebelliously. "No, that's not what this is all about. I think I'm being visited by the Devil."

Now that Bogges had made this statement, he found that he felt very badly indeed, nauseous, as though he were suffering an acute attack of vertigo. He sat down and wished he had something to drink.

"You look like you could do with some water," said Japrowski.

Japrowski was forced to go back to the men's to fetch it; the paper had long ago done away with the frivolous expense of maintaining a water cooler. To management's delight, abolishing the communal spot had produced the additional benefit of stifling collegiality. This tended to promote what the executive editor called creative tension. Japrowski returned shortly with a glass of the chemical vileness that flows through the District of Columbia's pipes. Bogges tried to drink without tasting what he was swallowing. He felt marginally better when he was finished.

"I take it you were joking, Eustace."

"No, yes, I'm not sure. You see, last night I had the same dream—that is, I dreamt of Dr. Fall. I'd been reading a Jesuit's paper on mental illness and diabolic possession before bed."

"Why in God's name were you reading that?"

"What did you read before you went to bed, Abel?"

"The 10-Q from an internet company that just went public. OK, I see what you mean. But don't you think the reason you dreamed about your devil was because you were reading about him?"

"That's what I thought when I woke up," replied Bogges.

"What changed your mind?"

Bogges found that he couldn't answer this question. The prospect of thinking it through was oppressive. "Maybe I'm losing my mind," Bogges said in lieu of thought.

"That's hard to say, Eustace. Opinion is pretty evenly divided between those who think you are already mad and those who think that it's a work in progress."

"Thanks."

"For goodness' sake, you know what people are like. They don't know what to make of you. My feeling is the world needs outsiders."

"There's not much point in being an outsider," said Bogges gloomily, "when the world won't leave you alone. Why don't we talk about something else?"

Japrowski also thought it was time to change the subject. "Miriam and I were hoping you would come to dinner Sunday."

"Thanks, I have a date." Bogges cursed himself for using the expression.

Japrowski beamed. "I'm glad to hear it. That should drive the demons from your soul. It's about time you started getting out. How long has it been since the divorce? Two years, isn't it?"

"Two years and five months."

"Know it to the minute, do you?"

"The alimony helped me keep track."

"Miriam and I always wondered what you saw in her."

"I saw what everyone could see."

"Did you have to marry, ah, what everyone can see?"

"I thought marriage would keep it all for me alone, and keep it available. I was mistaken."

"You are not the first man to make that mistake about marriage."

Japrowski looked wistful when he said this.

Bogges eyed his friend with sympathy. He considered Japrowski's wife. It shouldn't be altogether onerous to deny oneself the pleasures of Miriam's bony nakedness. That was Bogges's view. Japrowski probably held a different view. On the other hand, not finding a friend's wife desirable had a lot to be said for it. The two men remained silent, thinking, so far as they could recollect the experience, what life with sex was like. When memories of sensual vigor had been privately and separately gone over, Bogges said, "Sally's remarrying."

"Who's the lucky fellow?"

"Jonah Thomas."

"That will fix him. You may be dreaming about demons, but you have an angel looking after you."

"Thomas is giving her a column in Sunday Books."

Japrowski roared.

"It's not funny."

"Yes, it is Eustace, it is very funny. This may be JT's first career error."

"Do you really think so?" asked Bogges.

"We live in hope, my friend."

Japrowski left soon after this exchange, and Bogges turned to the mail. The first envelope he opened contained an invoice, in scarlet ink on midnight-blue paper, two sessions of psychotherapy at $300 per fifty minutes, from Dr. Fall. There was no return address, of course.

CHAPTER 4

"But no, Mr. Bogges, I can't give out the address," said the bank manager.

"Yet the money was taken from my account."

"According to your instructions, Mr. Bogges."

"I want to see these so-called instructions. Please," he remembered to say after a pause.

"If you'll just give me a minute, I'll bring it up on my screen."

"I suppose anyone can put anything on a computer screen. I want to see instructions on a piece of paper with my signature."

"We are a paperless operation."

"Then how will you know that what you find on your screen are my instructions?"

"It will be under your account number."

Bogges gave it up, for the moment, and waited for Ms. Celproh to finish tapping at her keyboard.

"Our system is so slow today," said Ms. Celproh with what she thought was a companionable, perhaps inviting, smile. Her large yellow teeth detracted from the effect, as did her exophthalmic glare. She turned back to her glowing screen. Whatever she was waiting for hadn't manifested itself. She drew back her lips, a tick of impatience, exposing more teeth, receding gums, dentine roots.

"Here we are, Mr. Bogges. Yes, everything is in order."

The bank manager treated Bogges to another toothy smile. Before Bogges could argue with her, the phone on the desk chirruped. She picked up the receiver, listened, said she would be right over, excused herself and left, neglecting to turn off the computer. Bogges watched through the glass wall of the cubicle as she walked across the lobby and disappeared into the vault. He got up and went around the desk to look at the computer screen. He ran his eye down a column of figures, deposits, withdrawals, a surprising number of fees. Toward the bottom of the screen were instructions to transfer $600 into the account of Dr. Grippin Fall, a series of numbers which Bogges assumed to belong somehow to the doctor, and then the name and address of a bank in Zurich. Bogges also saw that his account had been charged a further $50 for the transfer. He jotted down the information from the screen onto a scrap of paper, not that he thought it would get him anywhere, and went back to his chair. When Ms. Celproh returned, he told her he wanted the money refunded.

"I'm afraid that's impossible, Mr. Bogges. You'll have to take that up with Dr. Fall."

"I don't know how to reach Dr. Fall," said Bogges. "If you'd give me his address, I might be able to resolve the matter."

"The bank is very protective of its customers' privacy. It is absolutely against all our rules to release that information."

"What about my privacy? And my money?"

"I'm sorry I can't be of more help. I must say, it is most unusual to pay someone you can't locate."

"Those are my feelings, Madame. Doesn't that suggest to you that perhaps I didn't authorize this transaction?"

Ms. Celproh appeared unmoved, had become bored with the discussion. "Is there anything more I can do for you?" she said indifferently.

"You can't do more before you've done something."

"I beg your pardon," she said.

Bogges gritted his teeth. "Before you do more, you have to do something. After you've done something, then you can do more. Never mind. I want to close my account."

"I'm sorry you're not happy with our service."

"That's important to you, is it?"

"It's in our vision statement. We are a proactive bank, anticipating our customers' needs, providing service of the most valued kind."

"Good, splendid. I want my money in cash, the kind I value most, one dollar bills."

This got her attention in a way that none of the preceding had managed to do.

"You are not serious, Mr. Bogges."

"If you were serious about anticipating my needs, you'd know that I am."

"Well, it's a most unusual request. I don't know if we have that many singles on hand. You do realize you are withdrawing close to seven thousand dollars."

"It was more than seven before you gave my money away."

"According to your instructions, Mr. Bogges."

"Can you tell me when I issued these instructions?"

"Certainly."

Ms. Celproh did something with her keyboard. "Monday, September seventh." She looked up triumphantly and, to clinch it, "at 2:47 pm."

Bogges thought back to Monday afternoon. He had been asleep in his office, dreaming of Dr. Fall. He decided not to inform the bank manager. "Could I have my money now?"

"I'll see what I can do."

When Ms. Celproh returned, she was awkwardly carrying two canvas bags fastened at the top and without handles. "Six thousand, six hundred and sixty-six dollars, Mr. Bogges. If you'll sign, please."

"I thought it was six thousand, seven hundred and sixty-six."

"There's a hundred-dollar deposit for the two bags, refundable when you return the bank's property," she replied.

"You've done it again," said Bogges.

"I don't understand."

"You've disbursed my funds without my permission."

Ms. Celproh was puzzled. "It's only a deposit, Mr. Bogges."

"Call it what you like. I'm short a hundred dollars. Actually, I'm short that plus what you already gave away. I want it back."

"How will you carry all that money?"

"I'll give you a ten for that trash basket behind your desk."

"I can't sell you bank property, Mr. Bogges."

"I'll give you a dollar for the liner."

"I'll see if I can find you a shopping bag, Mr. Bogges."

In the event, the sixty-seven wads of singles required two large shopping bags. The bags were from a lingerie shop which sold sanitized commercial naughtiness.

"Will there be anything else, Mr. Bogges?"

Bogges only sighed. A disapproving guard unlocked the front door to let him out. It was past six o'clock, and the bank closed at five forty-five on Fridays. Bogges didn't pay much attention to the remarks of the two young men who fell into step behind him as he emerged from the bank. He'd gone several paces, had turned off commercial Wisconsin Avenue onto residential Dumbarton Street, when shouted words penetrated.

"Yo, dude, I'm talking to you!"

Bogges hunched his shoulders, gripped the shopping bags more firmly. The youths, wearing baggy overalls, sleeveless net shirts, combat boots, drew abreast.

"Been shopping for your girlfriend, fat man?"

Bogges quickened his pace.

"What's the big fucking hurry, man? You're going to give yourself a fucking heart attack," said the other.

Bogges glanced at the speaker. His head was shaven, except for a tuft of hair over a shallow, pimply forehead. The tuft had been greased, or glued, into a spike and dyed a greenish yellow, a unicorn in molt.

"Nah, he's going to have a fucking heart attack when his fucking girl-friend puts on that shit he bought her," said the first.

Bogges looked to his left. This one had a crewcut streaked orange and black. A brass ring pierced a porcine nostril. A skull and crossbones, finely etched, was tattooed on a large cleft chin. He was more muscular than the one on the right, who nevertheless also looked as though he lifted weights. Crewcut put his hand on a bag.

"Show us what she's going to wear."

"Maybe we should put it on her ourselves," said the other.

Bogges raised the shopping bags to breast height. He bent his arms and thrust out sharply, elbowing the thug on his left into an iron fence. The slighter thug went over the curb and fell into the street. The crewcut one had ricocheted off the fence. He appeared to be regaining his footing. The unicorn spike showed above the curb. Bogges braced himself. A sound like tap dancing distantly rapped out. It neared, and the noise became heavi-er, metal cleats on pavement, horseshoes clattering, hooves pounding. The young thug in the street had risen to his knees. The enormous black poodle with gaping maw and eyes aflame galloped down upon him. The beast passed, and passing swiped a massively clawed paw like an armored knight's mailed fist across the youth's neck. The head, practically severed, nodded over, and the blood came, a fountain spurting in the air, spray-ing and showering the second youth. A hunting knife he'd drawn from his belt fell to the sidewalk, and he ran calling and weeping back to the crowds on Wisconsin Avenue. The neck gave a last squirt, which coated the fallen knife. Bogges hoped the blood wouldn't wash off all the finger-prints, not that the police would much care after they'd apprehended the bloody screaming survivor. Bogges heard sirens. He moved on, confident that the poodle's master had the situation in hand. He wondered if the serrations on the knife would match the wounds the dog's paw had made; he wondered if the poodle and its master were one and the same being; he wondered why he wasn't more upset. He pursued his course home. Inside, he placed the shopping bags on the loaded mail table, took the ice bucket from the bar cart, and went down to the basement kitchen. Before he went back upstairs he remembered he'd want to dine at some point, bachelor weeknight meal. He'd recently discovered sauerkraut in a plastic bag lacked the tinny flavor of the canned version. He cut open a bag, a package of franks, and left them to stew together in a pot over a low flame. Seated in the green club chair which fitted him like a glove, drink in hand, he considered the afternoon's events. It seemed likely that Dr. Fall had been behind everything: the two thugs, the holdup, the animal executioner. They were all part of his therapy. But to what end? It was a question that answered itself. Bogges drank faster. He felt exhausted by the whole business. Empty glass in lap, he slept.

"I find that automatic payment is easier for all concerned, Mr. Bogges," said Dr. Fall. "I suggest you open another checking account at the earliest opportunity."

Dr. Fall was dressed in a blue three-piece suit with gray pinstripes, a banker's uniform, except for the black leather moccasins with fringe and tassels, which looked more like the footwear of a stockbroker. He was standing by the mail table, one small beringed hand resting on the first of the two shopping bags. He reached in and withdrew three hundred-dollar wads. He placed these inside his jacket.

"Of course," he said, "advance payment is always welcome."

He rested his elbow on the rifled bag and crossed one leg in front of the other, forefoot raised and balanced casually on its toes.

"If you recall," he went on conversationally, "we were talking about money at the end of our last session."

"I know who you are now," said Bogges by way of reply.

Dr. Fall looked amused. "And what does that mean to you?"

"You can stop pretending to be a psychiatrist."

"What would you like me to be?"

Bogges sighed. He reached down for his glass and with the gesture realized he was awake. "I'm not dreaming," he said, hearing his own voice in wonder. He looked over to where Dr. Fall had been leaning against the shabby mail table and saw in his place a graceful youth with enormous wings. The wings rose high above his head, brushing the ceiling and extending down to slender calves. The winged figure was nobly dressed, cloaked in the robes of an ancient philosopher. Hair, flesh, and wings were mauve, except where the feathers lay against each other and overlapped, producing darker, brownish highlights in the folds. A fiery sheen enveloped the youth, a glow that cast no light. His expression was impassive but without suggesting peace, rather the opposite. The eyes were bright red, the pupils, which were peculiarly enlarged, seemed to look out from a deep abyss. The look was both hungry and dead at the same time.

Bogges blinked, and Dr. Fall was back, perched like a gargoyle in a banker's pin-striped suit on the ledge before the dormer window.

"Must you crouch like that?" said Bogges irritably. He found some relief in his annoyance. It helped to cover up his fright.

Dr. Fall flexed his legs with an avian movement. They hung slightly angled several inches from the floor. This reminded Bogges how very small, how dwarfish, was Dr. Fall. The big head and pointed beard emphasized the disproportion of the stubby limbs. He looked more than ever like a gargoyle, now at ease.

"Money is a form of credit, Mr. Bogges. And credit is a form of honor. Money, being handier, has replaced the other forms. That's why the businessman is the most honored among your kind."

"Your kind," said Bogges excitedly. "You said your kind."

"And what does that mean to you?"

"You are not of my kind. You are another kind of being. You're Lucifer, Satan, Mephistopheles, The Devil, damn it."

"You have gone from believing I am an element of your dreams to believing I am an evil spirit. I suggest to you that this belief is part of a larger dream-world. You are making progress. I congratulate you. When you accept me simply as your therapist, then we shall truly begin our work together."

"Why have you singled me out. Why are you tormenting me?"

Dr. Fall smiled patiently. "I am not tormenting you, Mr. Bogges. It is what is inside you, what we bring to the surface together, that torments you. Moreover, I did not single you out. My patients come to me, and I make myself available provided, that is, that they are suitable cases for treatment."

"When did I come to you? I've never asked for your, your attention."

"Come, come, Mr. Bogges, denial will not help you. Why don't we say that you've been preparing yourself all your life for our encounters."

Bogges suddenly thought that denial might very well help him. "Our Father, who art in heaven, hallowed be Thy name," he began.

This was as far as he got. Dr. Fall interrupted with a look of contempt. "Don't think that will get you anywhere."

The moist red lips appeared to spit behind the little beard. The black hole of a mouth gaped. Then the jaws clamped shut with a sound of teeth against teeth. The mouth smiled, but the eyes retained a hard expression.

"A man of your intelligence," Dr. Fall said in an even tone, "must admit that to believe in the Devil, but not in God, is an untenable position. Or am I mistaken in thinking that you do not believe in God?"

Bogges hesitated. "I don't know."

"Quite so. But you believe in money. You believe that with it you can obtain what you desire, and, furthermore, you believe that it is desirable in itself."

"Why," asked Bogges helplessly, "are you talking about money?"

"Because there is nothing to which money is not relevant, Mr. Bogges. Money makes the world go round."

The cliché got Bogges over the rest of his fright.

"I'm not interested," he said.

"I think you are." Dr. Fall sniggered.

The snigger somehow reminded Bogges of a little boy peering through the keyhole of the girls' bathroom, secure in the knowledge that no one could see him. He was fairly certain he hadn't been that boy.

Dr. Fall stared at Bogges. "Yes, I think you are interested. Who is not interested in money? It holds mankind's greatest secrets, and it reveals them! One might say that what people do in private, money does in public."

Bogges stared back. "Money," he said, "was invented as a medium of exchange to facilitate trade."

"A perfect textbook description, but insipid," replied Dr. Fall. "The truth is never insipid, I assure you. Money, of all things, was not invented for such a dull, sensible, plausible use. It was born of love, in ancient Lydia, in the king's bedroom, in Sardis.

"This king, Candaules, had a strange fancy. He was in love with his wife and thought her the most beautiful creature in the world. Now, there was a favorite in his court, a fellow called Gyges. To him, Candaules would confide all his hopes and plans and, above all things, he would celebrate the beauty of his wife, the queen.

"It is unnatural for a king to be so devoted to one woman. To be king is to possess, at least potentially, all women. In that way, money and king-ship resemble each other. Because the king had done violence to his own nature, his natural sentiments turned on him. He told Gyges one day that he wished him to see the queen's person in all the glory of her nakedness. His excuse was that Gyges must be convinced of the queen's beauty. Gyges protested. He pleaded with Candaules not to expose the privacy of this most personal treasure lest its value be stolen. Candaules insisted. Once the voyeur, and its counterpart, the lust to expose oneself, are prodded into life, there's no stopping either. Narcissus himself was no more excited by his own reflection than was Candaules anticipating the public undressing of his queen. That night, Gyges hid behind the door of the royal bedroom. Candaules lay on the marital couch, a magnificent piece of furniture, feet of solid gold in the shape of lions' heads, ivory panels depicting the labors of Hercules, silken coverlets dyed a brilliant orange-saffron; he lay naked and engorged. The queen entered. She turned her back to Candaules and removed her golden tiara. Her hair fell to her shoulders. She lifted her purple robe, circular in the Persian manner, over her head and put it on a low chair facing Gyges's hiding place. In the yellow light of the oil lamps, her flesh was smooth, shining, iridescent, nacreous. She turned and ap-proached the couch. Gyges slipped out of the room. The lamps flickered with his passage. The queen was no fool. She didn't scream. She didn't turn her head. She joined the king. Secretly, she was excited too. The next morning she called for Gyges. Her most trusted attendants, Amazons of great strength, stood by her side. The crescent-shaped brands on their cheeks showed they were slaves of the Moon. Gyges suspected nothing. The queen would often consult him. When he entered her private chamber, she told him that he must either assassinate the king and marry her or die on the spot. The Amazons, to help concentrate his mind, brandished their javelins."

"What," interrupted Bogges, "does this have to do with money?"

"Everything. Gyges strangled Candaules. He died like a dog. Gyges married the queen and founded a dynasty which ended with Croesus."

"Rich as Croesus," said Bogges.

"Exactly. For it was Croesus's grandfather, Sadyattes, who invented money. It happened this way. In the time of Sadyattes, the common folk were giving birth exclusively to daughters, the nobles exclusively to sons. You can see the difficulty. The usual prayers were given. In their hundreds, cattle were slaughtered until the hands of the priests were too weary to hold the knife. Burnt offerings were made until the air was rank and foul, and the sleep of the king was troubled. I daresay his sleep was made uneasy by the stink in his nostrils as much as by his worries. Nevertheless, the king did sleep, and in his sleep there came to him a dream, sent by Apollo and delivered by Hermes."

"Which one were you?" said Bogges nastily.

"Please don't interrupt, Mr. Bogges. The God-sent dream was a shimmer of gold, a vision of shining yellow roundels which fell like rain on the fields and groves and vineyards of Lydia. And the fields and groves and vineyards became fertile and bore fruit, olive and grape and grain, a bountiful crop. And in his dream, Sadyattes feasted with his people, and the people grew fat. When Sadyattes awoke, he understood the portent of his dream: he must shower gold on his people, gold in the form of roundels, of discs, of coin. He ordered that all those who possessed golden implements, cups and plates, urns and tripods—the possessions of the nobles, in other words—must turn them over to a Royal Mint. In return, the newly established mint would give back an equal weight in gold coin with the head of a lion incised on one side, a bow and an arrow on the other. He further commanded that these signs, sacred to Artemis the Virgin Huntress, made the coins and their purpose sacred too. He then secretly ordered the Priestess of Artemis to declare that the daughters of the poor might prostitute themselves until they collected a sufficient dowry of coin to marry, and that once this sum was earned they would regain their purity in the Artemision, the sacred Temple of Artemis. Naturally, the youth of the nobility were eager to enjoy the favors of the maidens. Later, they were similarly eager to regain their gold."

"A very amusing story," said Bogges.

"I'm so glad you're amused. I had hoped you would find the story instructive. Please try to concentrate, Mr. Bogges. Human consciousness came to be during an episode of suicidal narcissism. Narcissism's counterparts, self-exposure and voyeurism, gave birth to money. This is the progress of mankind."

Dr. Fall made this pronouncement with satisfaction. Nevertheless, he seemed disconcerted, as though Bogges had somehow disappointed him. Dr. Fall shook his head. Then he stood up and made for the door.

"Money," said Dr. Fall with his hand on the knob, "was invented so that man might take part in the here and now in a new, more vivid, more satisfying way. Let me refer you for further reflection to the story of Croesus and Solon in Herodotus."

"Aren't you going to vanish in a puff of smoke?" asked Bogges.

Dr. Fall turned to him. "And a clap of thunder and a sulfurous stench? Do you really think all that is necessary?"

"So you could do it if you wanted to? Just the way you sent that poodle to kill the mugger. And who was that winged figure I saw?"

Dr. Fall laughed. "I don't know. Why don't you describe him for me."

"You know very well what I saw, a youth in robes with huge wings. He was dark red, and his eyes were inflamed."

"It sounds like the miniature in a manuscript of St. Gregory Nazianzen, I'd say offhand."

"A miniature of what?"

"Oh, a fanciful portrait of Satan. They imagined all sorts of things at the end of the Roman empire. Now, I think you have enough to work on until our next session. Au revoir."

The door slammed behind Dr. Fall with a clap that made the frame shiver. After a while, Bogges went into his little study in back of the parlor and looked on the shelves for Herodotus. When he'd found him, he searched for the reference Dr. Fall had given. He discovered a previously overlooked underlining in his secondhand copy. He found an eraser and applied it. Some people make a book their own by marking it with a pencil; Bogges made it his own with an eraser. He came across the story of Candaules and Gyges, more or less the way Dr. Fall had told it. Herodotus also seemed to think the Lydians had invented coinage. There was nothing about Sadyattes's dream, although Herodotus confirmed the bit about the common folk's daughters prostituting themselves before marriage. Bogges seemed to have gotten to the end of Croesus's life. He turned back. The Solon story was near the beginning. It appeared that Solon was a wise man from Athens on a tour. When he came to Sardis, Croesus showed off his vast treasures and asked the wise man who was the happiest among mortals, evidently expecting Solon to name him. Instead, Solon named several obscure Greeks who had done their duty and died doing it, the point being that no one can be called happy until you know how he ends up. Croesus decided that Solon was a fool. This seemed to Bogges a reasonable judgment.

Bogges sniffed. A sulfurous stench was coming up from the kitchen. He remembered the franks and sauerkraut and went downstairs to turn off the flame.

CHAPTER FIVE

"No, I never know when he's going to show up."

"Has anyone else seen him?" asked Marina gently.

"No. You don't believe me, do you?"

"I'm Catholic. The nuns who taught me saw the Devil a lot more frequently than they saw God."

Bogges sighed. "I guess that qualifies me to become a nun."

He leaned over from his pouf, a sort of fat cushion on the floor which he had had difficulty settling onto and would have greater difficulties getting up from. He took a sip of the wretched honey wine, Tej, Ethiopian nectar the menu called it. It tasted like something mixed up from flat soda pop and cleaning fluid, not that he had ever drunk either of those. Nor had he ever eaten Ethiopian food. He seemed to be able to get the meat in the buttery yellow sauce down. The red chili barbecue mess was another matter, as was the spongy pancake it was served on in place of plate and eating utensils and bread or rice or pasta or any other proper starch. As a rule, Bogges stayed away from third-world cuisines. This venture into the unknown was Marina's idea. At least the portions were small. Evidently, one was supposed to fill up on the pancakes; grayish-white, cold, limp, moist, they reminded him of dishtowels in need of laundering. The loud table of Ethiopians next to him became still louder. He looked over. They managed the lack of fork and knife better than he did; it looked like manners. Bogges remembered his.

"I'm glad you enjoyed the concert, Marina."

"Nicholas Rasumosky's playing was heavenly."

Rasumosky had been the soloist. Bogges did not share Marina's opinion of the playing. Even the musician's gestures had been annoying. He couldn't seem to hold still, swaying and scraping and bowing, emoting as though the music couldn't speak for itself.

"I'd never had a chance to hear Pleyel before," said Marina. "He was a pupil of Mozart's, did you know?"

"Yes, I saw it on the program."

In fact, the program noted that Pleyel in his time had been said to wear the mantle of his teacher, along with a lot of other nonsense about the concerto. Bogges thought that Pleyel was the heir to Mozart in the sense that a degenerate son is heir to a gifted father. Pleyel had less to say than the master and used a lot more notes to say it. Bogges shifted his knees uncomfortably, and the straw tripod or platform that held the platter of food shook and trembled, slopping sauce in no particular direction, like Pleyel's music.

Marina returned to the subject they'd been discussing since they'd sat down.

"Are you frightened?" she asked.

"Strangely enough, I'm not. You see, I don't feel possessed. I don't feel that I'm being made to do things I don't want to, except for listening to him and having him there, of course. He just visits me, if you see what I mean. I guess, though, if he's really the Devil, that will change; he'll grow more assertive."

"Perhaps, perhaps not. That might make you more assertive, you know, stronger, more willing to fight him off. I think he's trying to seduce you. These stories he's telling you, they must have some purpose."

"I suppose," Bogges replied. "But I can't think what that purpose is."

"He wants your soul, Eustace."

"Yes, I understand that that's the traditional objective, but how does he think telling stories and pretending to be a psychiatrist will achieve that?"

"I don't know. Do you find what he says interesting?"

"Yes."

"Do you want to hear more of his stories?"

"Yes and no."

"I think it's always safer to just say no, Eustace. Yes and no is dangerous."

Bogges thought Marina was probably right. While he searched for something else to say, he watched their waitress clear the neighboring table. She was tall and slender. Her features might have been carved from a block of smooth ebony, high cheekbones, large black eyes, graceful nose as noble as a hawk's; the Ethiopian women in the restaurant were handsome. This one might have been the Queen of Sheba, and lucky for Solomon if that's what she'd looked like. Bogges thought about asking Dr. Fall the next time he made an appearance.

"You are expecting him to visit you again, aren't you?"

Bogges found it difficult to admit. He made himself say yes.

"I think you should go see Father Roche."

"Who's that?"

"My priest."

"I'm not a Catholic, Marina."

"That won't matter to him. In fact, it doesn't matter to the Church."

"Why's that?"

"She's the only institution that still believes in Satan. One of her jobs, her mission, is to root him out wherever he's found, even in an unbeliever."

"This priest of yours, is he French?"

"Yes, but he's lived here for years. He ministers to the French community. His English is very good, perfect really. He has no accent."

"I'll think about it," said Bogges, thinking he'd rather treat with the Devil he knew than a Frenchman he didn't.

"You know," said Marina with a smile, "when my father said he'd think about it, he meant no. Really, Eustace, I think you'd like Father Roche. He's a very clever man. You should have heard his sermon this morning. It was called 'La peur qui engendre ses complexités vagabondes.'"

"My French isn't that good; something about fear and complexity was it?"

"Yes. Father Roche translated it as the fear which engenders feckless nugacities."

Bogges burst out laughing. "What a mouthful!"

"It sounds better in French," Marina admitted.

"But what does it mean?" asked Bogges.

"That fear leeches meaning from life, makes it aimless, empty, and fraught."

"A lot of things do that," he replied. "Boredom, say, and loneliness, they seem to me much more effective in making life meaningless than fear. After all, when you're afraid, you're living pretty intensely."

"I think that's more a chemical reaction," she answered. "Father Roche was talking about a spiritual condition. In his view, fear is opposed to love."

"I thought hate was the opposite of love," said Bogges.

"No, hate is the perversion of love. It's a perverse love. That's why hatred belongs to Satan, the perverse angel. Fear is the absence of love, a nothingness. Can't you see," she said suddenly with shining eyes, "that the world came into being from a vast outpouring of love?"

Bogges had come across similar observations in his reading. It was altogether another thing to hear someone actually say it. Bogges thought that if the someone saying it had been anyone other than Marina he would have instantly shown by irrefutable proofs that the recent activities of, say, Al Qaeda, or the somewhat more distant gestures of Nazi Germany or Stalin's Russia or Napoleonic France or the Golden Horde, and so on, suggested rather that the world was an outpouring of hate. Whether that included fear was merely a quibble. On the other hand, Marina radiated such warmth and solicitude, and was so attractive doing it, Bogges could just imagine, in Marina's presence, that she had a point. For a moment he had a rapturous vision of Marina as love personified, female incarnate. He wondered how he could ever have compared her beauty to that of a monkey's. Then Dr. Fall's version of Eve came back to him. Bogges looked at his companion as though to erase Dr. Fall's story, and she was just Marina again. He sighed to himself.

"The evidence is against it," he said.

"Oh, evidence," said Marina. "I don't give a damn for your evidence. I'm talking about fact, the one, true, real fact that you can experience."

"I take it you've experienced this fact." .

"God's love, or rather the fact that God is love? Certainly. Why else would anyone pray?"

"Usually people pray to ask for things, that's my understanding. It's a transaction in which God plays the part of a philanthropic department-store owner who hands over the goods after a certain amount of begging and haggling."

"You don't really believe that, Eustace."

"Of course not. I was describing what most people who pray seem to mean by prayer."

"I think that people are always praying for the presence of God, whether they know it or not."

"That is very kind of you."

"Oh, Eustace, you are impossible."

"I often think that myself."

"Do you know," said Marina, "I think what I like most about you is what an adolescent you are. Imagine, wondering what you're all about at your age."

"Marina," said Bogges forcefully, "let me assure you, I wonder what other people are about a lot more."

"That's the journalist in you," she said dismissively.

"There are worse things," Bogges said with less force.

Marina tore off a piece of pancake and with the same hand scooped up vegetable and meat. Then she did something complicated with her thumb, fore, and middle fingers. This produced a neat package which she put whole in her mouth. Either she was an habitué or it was some chef's skill. To change the subject, Bogges inquired how she did it.

"I just watched what the people next to us were doing."

"Oh. Show me how to do it."

Marina demonstrated the maneuver.

"Your three fingers are working independently of each other," he said.

"I never thought about it. I suppose they are. Is that hard?"

"I can't do it."

"Try without thinking about it," she said.

Bogges didn't think he could do anything without thinking about it. He didn't think anyone else could either, but he was willing to be proved wrong. The first thing, obviously, was to make his mind blank. The question then arose whether he should think about nothing or, alternatively, empty his mind. Thinking about nothing, he thought, might be a kind of thinking, like watching television or listening to pop music. With this thought, he tried to empty his mind. A series of other thoughts then passed through on their way out. It occurred to him that the new critics were like the physicians of earlier times. They both have theory; the theory requires bleeding. When the patient is emptied of blood, he's pronounced cured. Only the relatives notice he's also dead. Deconstructionists perform similar operations on literature. He realized that emptying one's mind was very much like taking out the garbage. He remembered that for the five years he'd been married, Sally had not once taken out the garbage. However, she would make the bed, something else he hadn't done all weekend. He thought about going to bed himself. He thought about going to bed with Marina. He wondered if this were possible. He found that his mind was pleasantly empty. He reached for a pancake. The name *Injera*, what the Ethiopians apparently called the stuff, came to mind. This set him to thinking about Plato's theory of the onomatopoeic origins of language. It was as good a notion as any. *Injera* (noun): unwashed dishtowel when masticated. How did the caveman tell their women they were going to hunt mastodon? Obviously, by trumpeting. But how did one get from making trumpeting noises to saying *elephant*? He remembered that Marina's little boy, when he was learning to talk, would say *efenant*. He thought it was a better word than *heffalump* in *Winnie the Pooh*; it got the tusks in somehow. *Winnie the Pooh* suggested to him that this was probably as empty as his mind was likely to get. He scooped food and twiddled his fingers without thinking much about what they were doing. The food went flying; the injera fell limply to his lap.

"Would you like me to do it for you?" asked Marina.

"No, thank you. I'm not very hungry. I'd like a napkin, though."

"I don't think they have those. Here, use this injera."

Bogges wiped at his pants. The smear blended not very noticeably with his khakis.

"I could let the babysitter go early," said Marina. "Would you like to come home with me, and I'll make you something?"

"Won't Hugo be waiting for you?" Hugo was Marina's child.

"He's been asleep since eight-thirty."

"Good God. Is he sick?"

"Eustace, he's only four. That's his bedtime."

"If you don't think it's too much trouble," said Bogges, "there's nothing I'd like better."

Bogges suddenly found himself disconcerted, surprised by his own eagerness. He adjusted his features. Marina was giving him an interested look, not wary, not inviting, a plain look with a hint of speculation.

"Are you sure it's not too much trouble?" he repeated.

"It's not like you to be shy, Eustace." Marina now looked amused. "Tell me, are you planning something?"

"I don't know."

"Well, when you do, let me know, will you?"

"You'll be the first to know," said Bogges.

"I'm sure I will. Shall we get the check?"

With the change came wet paper towels wrapped in foil. Bogges wished this had come before he'd put his sticky hand in his pocket for his wallet, but he was still glad to get one. Outside, a gaunt madman, stripped to the waist, was directing a car into a parking-space. His naked chest, matted, streaked with perspiration, gleamed in the muggy night. His eyes shone no less than the neon of the Latino nightclub that appeared to be the destination of the young couple in the smart convertible. While the driver worked the wheel, the madman swooped and flapped and gamboled; he held up his hands and beckoned with them, he clapped, and made signs of approval and dismay, of delight and despair, acting out the drama of squeezing a car into a narrow space or, perhaps, caricaturing it. The madman darted in front of the car when it nosed forward and raced around behind when it backed in. The slick young man behind the wheel slammed his fist into the horn. The blast seemed to subdue the madman. He withdrew to the curb. When the couple emerged from the car, the madman held out his hand.

"Get the hell out of the way," said the young man.

"I been saving this space for you, man. I been guardin' it. An' while you gone, I be guardin' that pretty car. So that nuthin' bad be happen' to it."

He held out his hand again and rubbed his thumb against his forefinger. Bogges now perceived that the slick young man was his fellow editor Jonah Thomas and that his stylish companion was Sally Benton.

"Are you threatening me?" asked Thomas threateningly.

Bogges felt that he could not allow Thomas to act in a sensible manner. Nor could he allow Thomas to look heroic. Bogges pulled out his wallet and found a dollar bill.

"Here," he said to the madman, "go down to the corner, would you, and flag a cab."

The madman took the bill with alacrity and disappeared down the street.

"Christ, Eustace," said Thomas, "what makes you think a taxi is going to stop for that jerk?"

"I don't for a moment think a taxi will stop. It seemed to me that a dollar was a small price to pay for saving you from embarrassment. And how are you, Sally? May I introduce Marina Niemalle. This is Sally Benton and Jonah Thomas."

The two women eyed each other in the way people do who sense that one of them is about to make a bad bargain. Thomas looked at Marina indifferently and turned back to Bogges.

"What makes you think I was going to be embarrassed?" said Thomas.

"Well, to save the ladies from embarrassment," replied Bogges with smooth condescension.

Sally Benton pursed thin lips, and her expression, so far as could be discerned beneath her makeup, hardened. Bogges was enjoying her dilemma. She would have liked to have seen Thomas knock down the pest, would have watched without a trace of embarrassment. To admit this, however, might be construed as unladylike. Sally smiled. She tossed her blond hair. Her blue eyes widened. She half extended her hand, limp at the wrist, a gesture of greeting.

"I'm so pleased to meet you, Miss Niemalle." She said this in a dime-store southern accent. She was technically from the south. She'd grown up in northern Virginia, suburb of Washington; what real southerners call the occupied south. She turned graciously to Bogges.

"Well, Eustace, after all these years. Once we were man and wife. Now we are professional colleagues. What do you think of that?"

Marina came to Bogges's rescue. "I've heard a lot about you. It must have been so hard to let him go."

Bogges laughed. "I think Sally managed to get over it eventually. Oh, and congratulations, I understand you and Jonah are getting married."

"My, how word does get around. I do hope you all will attend our nuptials."

Despite the magnolia-scented accent, Bogges thought this was a somewhat New Age invitation: one of the major things to be said for divorce, in Bogges's view, was not to have to go on pretending at friendship. However, this apparently didn't let him off being polite.

"When is the ceremony?" asked Bogges.

"Oh, Eustace, you bad thing, you're still not opening your mail, are you? It's two weeks from next Saturday, which you'd know if you ever went through that awful mail table of yours. I bet our invitation has been just languishing there for days and days."

This was no doubt true. Bogges opened enough mail at the office; opening it at home was too much like work—that and the fact that his mail, aside from a few periodicals, consisted of bills and junk. He couldn't remember the last time he'd received an actual letter. Of course, he couldn't remember the last time he'd written one, aside from S. J. Chakravarti's. He would have liked to tell Sally to mind her own business. He didn't think he could get away with that. He decided he could get away with tormenting her by telling a story.

"There was a correspondent for one of the London papers back in the fifties," said Bogges, "who only opened his mail once a year. From time to time he would get dunning phone calls. Unlike the mail, he found these more difficult to avoid. It's said that he told a particularly persistent creditor that every year at Christmas he put all his bills into a trash basket, stirred them with a stick, fished out half a dozen, and promptly paid them." Bogges paused for dramatic effect. "He then informed this creditor that if he continued to harass him, he would not be in the next year's lottery."

Only Marina laughed.

"Ah can't understand"—Sally's accent had grown thicker for some reason—"why that man didn't pay his bills when they were due. It's downright discourteous. Think of all those poor storekeepers. Don't they have to live too?"

"That's a very good point, Sally," said Thomas. "And why would they go on extending credit to a deadbeat?"

"Well, I think he must have paid all his bills eventually," said Bogges.

'That's not clear from your story," replied Thomas in his editorial voice.

"It was an anecdote," said Bogges, now belligerent.

"What's that supposed to mean?" asked Thomas.

"An anecdote," Bogges said, "is a narrative that is striking in itself."

"I know what an anecdote is. What's the point? You apparently can't be bothered to open your mail, unless you're paid to do it. Is that the point?"

Bogges acknowledged to himself that this was a pretty good point. Just because Thomas was distasteful did not mean he wasn't clever. Being clever might even help in being distasteful, or vice versa. This thought would bear further examination. Meanwhile, Thomas must be stopped before he became altogether unmanageable.

"There are a number of possible views on the matter," said Bogges in his most sententious manner. "Duty requires us to open our mail. The demands of the world must be met. Granted, bills must be paid so that commerce may flourish; social obligations must be fulfilled so that intercourse among mankind may continue. This is the functioning of the hive. Once, however, was a time when people wrote letters. Their aim was to share their experience of life with friends. No one writes letters anymore, of course. Possibly, people no longer have experiences worth communicating. Possibly, people no longer have experiences worth having. Travel, for example, was once a great subject of letter-writing. Not anymore. There is no travel because there is no experience of people and place. You're crushed into a metal tube with several hundred other miserable specimens and hurled into the air. You can't see anything because you're going too fast and too high. You can't talk for the same reason. People once opened their mail for enchantment and delight. I can't see that the mail provides anything but onerous demands. I suppose people do go through their mail out of idle curiosity, but, really, it is the idlest of curiosity. Catalogues and circulars and fliers and coupons offering what no one in their right mind wants because no one in their right mind needs. It is ignoble to open the mail, that is, unless you're in a position to edit it."

"So I had it right," said Thomas. "You only open the mail you're paid to open."

"I am the alchemist who turns dull lead to gleaming gold."

At this moment a cab, no more ramshackle than should be expected, pulled up before the party, and the madman emerged. He held the door open and waved in Bogges and Marina triumphantly, regally. Bogges was as astonished as Thomas. Marina said goodnight and what a pleasure it was and slipped into the cab. Bogges felt obliged to give the madman another dollar.

"Lead to gold, lead to gold," said Bogges to Thomas and Sally, gesturing at the madman. He was able to close the door before either Thomas or Sally could respond. The reek of the madman inside the cab was strong. Bogges struggled with the window while giving directions.

"Window no open," said the driver, looking over his shoulder. "Window broken. I have air."

"We don't," said Bogges.

"No, no, from air-conditioning. See?" The driver pointed to a vent.

"It's not blowing back here," said Bogges.

"I fix." The driver fiddled with a dial, and a feeble breath stirred the back.

They got underway, and for a few minutes there was nothing but the whirr of the air conditioner and the only slightly less unimpressive growl of the engine. As they approached the Duke Ellington Bridge, which separated them from the wealthier, less interesting part of town, a harsh rumble erupted from the dash, followed quickly by metallic raspings. These grew in volume and seemed to extend forward, deeper into the hood. The driver wrenched at the air-conditioning regulator, but whatever had been set in motion was now pursuing its own course. Clankings briefly punctuated a drawn-out rasping sound. Then some essential part gave voice to a machined whine, a final groan, silence. The cab rolled to a stop midway on the bridge.

"Gold seems to have turned back into lead," said Marina.

"You wait. I fix," said the driver. He got out of the cab, lifted up the hood, disappeared from view.

"I'm beginning to lose confidence in our chauffeur," said Bogges.

"I don't think he's the problem," Marina replied. "I think it's the engine."

"Should we walk the rest of the way?" asked Bogges.

"All right."

The driver didn't notice them leave. Bogges briefly contemplated giving him something for his trouble, decided against. The park below the bridge in the late summer night exhaled green odors neither fresh nor tired: mossy, scented with decay, fecund. Bogges took Marina's arm. As they crossed the bridge, Bogges wondered in a focused manner what Marina would give him to eat. Marina wondered in a not very definite way what it would be like to have all that weight on top of her. Then Bogges began to wonder what it would be like to hold Marina under him, and Marina began to think about what she might prepare for Bogges's supper. These thoughts brought them in silence to the door of Marina's building. Marina fumbled in her purse for her keys.

"I have vitello tonnato," she said as she let them in.

"Good. What is it?"

"Cold loin of veal with a tuna anchovy mayonnaise."

"It sounds wonderful."

"I can warm up some macaroni alla Siciliana if you'd rather."

"How about both?"

The TV was blaring across the apartment. Bogges wondered how Hugo could sleep with the noise and why didn't the babysitter turn it off when Marina asked her how the child's evening had gone. Perhaps the sitter hadn't noticed that it was on; that would explain why it was so loud. Marina and the sitter began to discuss Hugo's activities. Marina had a friendly but intent expression as she questioned the girl. She seemed to be listening to the inflection of the answers as much as the words themselves, as though there were some essence or aspect of Hugo's being that had to be gauged and measured, that the health of his developing spirit no less than his body could be determined by an account of his dinner, his bath, his bedtime. The sitter, young and heavily mascaraed, had very white, grainy skin. She wore a bright smile but told her story with an air of indifference. Bogges turned his attention from the discussion to the TV. There, two women a little older than the sitter were arguing. They had the open-eyed look of people who get plenty of exercise and rarely are troubled by thought. But something was troubling them now, Bogges couldn't quite make out what, money possibly. A moment later it was revealed as sex. The dispute revolved around the question of whether oral sex constituted a breach of faith, the fellating woman having performed the act on some partner other than her fiancée. Her position seemed to be that what she had done was done without arousal, a benevolent thank-you for a pleasant evening out, no more. The second girl maintained that she too had performed sexual acts in various forms without arousal but that nevertheless any of these was no less sexual than another and that her feelings, or lack of, were irrelevant. She somewhat caustically added that her feelings had also been irrelevant to her partners. Bogges thought there was something to be said for both points of view, perhaps all three. He was also mildly surprised at the subject matter, but then he hadn't watched much TV in the last few decades or so. Marina had satisfied herself concerning Hugo's routine, was paying the sitter and showing her out.

"Eustace, if you're going to watch TV while I get your supper would you at least turn it down?"

"No," he said reluctantly; he had wanted to know how the argument would develop. "I'll sit with you in the kitchen."

"Fine. Just give me a minute to check on Hugo."

The TV was now broadcasting an advertisement for female lubricant. Bogges hadn't known there were such things. He found the ad almost as interesting as the show he'd been watching. When Marina came back, Bogges had had time to learn that the lubricant was called Pneumatica and that it was guaranteed; what precisely it was guaranteed to do, however, was too allusive for Bogges to pin down. He would have liked also to have known the name of the show, so far unrevealed. He had an idea he might tune in. But he turned off the TV and followed Marina into the kitchen; he thought he'd just run through the channels next week until he found it, not knowing that his cable company now provided him with 800 channels because he hadn't bothered to open the cancellation form that had come in the mail. The bill for this, when he got around to opening it, would come as a surprise. Bogges took a seat at the kitchen table beneath an arrangement of serious-looking copper pots hanging from some kind of turntable suspended from the ceiling. He watched Marina reach up for one of these and saw how her breast rounded under her blouse with the motion. This seemed to him the most suggestive and at the same time most innocently beautiful sight, image of bounty, the cook's bust. He held out his hands.

"Marina, come here."

He watched the arm descend, the breast hide itself in the folds of cloth, and the woman come over like a lamb to sit on his lap. He kissed her awkwardly.

"Not like that. It's a question of angles," she said.

Marina shifted her hardly noticeable weight and took Bogges by the chin. When she had things adjusted, her mouth surprised him with its softness. This experience went on for some time, although not nearly long enough from Bogges's point of view, when a small, high voice interrupted the proceedings.

"Why are you sitting on that man's lap, Mommy?"

Marina disengaged. She got up without smoothing her hair or her blouse, without any sign of being disconcerted, and went over to a chair at the other side of the table. The small boy, barefoot, clad in midnight-blue pajamas ornamented with silver crescent moons and various stars, climbed onto her lap. When he had snuggled in, he repeated his question.

"Are you comfy, darling?" she replied.

"Uhmm."

"I was just snuggling like you, sweetheart."

The boy considered this. "But you were kissing," he said.

Marina kissed her son. "And now I'm kissing you."

Hugo stared into the middle distance. Bogges couldn't determine whether the child was still considering, thinking of something else or, perhaps, remembering other times he had surprised his mother in similar situations.

"How are you, Hugo?" he said.

The child focused his gaze on Bogges. There was a pause, then, "Pleased to meet you, although it is past my bedtime."

Hugo delivered his speech in a distracted voice. He was thinking of something else. He screwed up his small features; his face took on a look of concentration. "If there's a road in the forest," he began in a sing-song, "and no one made it, where does it go?"

It was Bogges's turn to consider. "Well, there's lots of things that look like paths or trails in the woods. I guess they're just made by the wind, maybe by the animals who live there."

"But," said Hugo, "if you built a house at the end of the path, then it would go somewhere, wouldn't it?"

"Yes, it would," said Bogges.

"And if the house had a dog and cat, and the person who lived there was lost, and couldn't find his way home because the wind was blowing and covered up the path with leaves, then the dog could sniff and the cat could see in the dark and they could lead you home."

The child gave a great smile of satisfaction at the thought of his perfect household. Bogges admired the logic. Marina, having heard such speculations before, seemed less impressed.

"I want you to say goodnight to Mr. Bogges, Hugo."

"I'm hungry. I want a goodnight snack."

Marina looked at Bogges inquiringly. He tried to smile an indulgent smile. Marina quickly put together the meal, which Hugo shared with increasing boisterousness. The late hour, which weighed more and more heavily on Bogges, seemed only to stimulate Hugo to greater imaginative efforts.

"There was once a little dog named Toby," announced the child. "He didn't like oatmeal."

"I don't like oatmeal either," said Bogges politely.

Hugo looked gleefully back at Bogges. "I hate oatmeal!"

"Finish your macaroni, Hugo, and I'll tuck you in," said Marina.

Hugo picked a tube from his plate with a now thoroughly cheese-egg-plant-tomato-encrusted hand. He inspected this object and placed it in the center of his mouth. He then proceeded to draw air through it while pushing out his chin and lower lip. This made him look suddenly like a shrunken member of some disreputable club devoted to smoking exotic substances.

"Hugo, stop that, you'll choke," said his mother.

Hugo took the macaroni from his mouth and put it back on his plate. "The boy who owned Toby didn't like oatmeal too."

Bogges wondered without much interest where this was leading.

"But one day his mother made a big big bowl. So the little boy put Toby in the oatmeal and baked him in the oven."

And that, thought Bogges, was the end of Toby. However, Hugo wasn't finished.

"But this was magical. There was a great big explosion and the oven opened up and out jumped Toby the Oatmeal Dog."

Marina stood up. "That's quite enough, young man."

"But now Toby the Oatmeal Dog can talk and fly and do magic."

"You can tell me about it in the morning."

"Will he be here, too?" said Hugo pointing at Bogges.

Bogges took this as his cue to get up. "I'm afraid it's my bedtime too, Hugo. Thank you for the story. The next time, you can tell me what Toby does with his magical oatmeal powers."

Hugo looked approvingly at Bogges and held out his hand. "Pleased to meet you," he repeated, this time with enthusiasm.

Bogges laughed and shook the little hand gravely. "Thank you, Marina, for dinner, the concert, a most pleasant evening."

CHAPTER SIX

A beggar had installed himself and his worldly goods on the bench at the bus stop. Bogges supposed he should call him a homeless person. On the other hand, the beggar did seem to be living there. A plea pencilled on a strip of cardboard requested money for beer. No pupils showed in the beggar's eyes. The empty whites gave the man a far-seeing look. The beggar winked at Bogges. Bogges decided to give him a dollar, but at that moment his bus came and he thought better of it. As he stepped up to the platform, the beggar snarled something; it sounded like *have a nice day*. Bogges turned back and saw pupiled eyeballs roll down into their customary position. The appropriate quote came to him. He recited in a loud voice:

See the blind beggar dance, the cripple sing,
The sot a hero, lunatic a king.

The doors closed before he could see how the beggar took this. Still, Mondays didn't usually begin so well. He found a seat under the irritating poster about being part of the problem if you weren't part of the solution. The poster had been vandalized. He took a closer look. Someone had scrawled across it *Mind Your Own Business*.

At the paper, Saturday's mail was stacked in the hallway in front of his office. He unlocked the door, picked up the emptied waste basket and the letters. There would be time to go through some of it before the 11:00 meeting Morrow-Graves held with his editors at the beginning of every week.

The first letter, from Charlotte O'Sneade of Annandale, began, "I was just minding my own business ..." Bogges crumpled this up and threw it in the direction of the wastebasket. The next letter began with a variation on the tag. It followed its predecessor. A letter from the chairman of the Republican National Committee next caught attention.

"At the end of the day, the bottom line going forward is ..."

Bogges began to crumple up this one too and then reluctantly put it aside for publication. It was policy that the banal must be taken seriously if someone prominent commits it. Bogges glanced at the clock. There was time for a couple more if he didn't read them too carefully or all the way through. The envelope that came to hand was cream colored, heavy paper with a high linen content, a pleasure to hold and touch. The name and address were printed in Edwardian Script. The lettering was raised. The correspondent's name was familiar, J. Leftowitz Frisell. Bogges seemed to remember that he'd been U.N. ambassador or something similar.

"Our tripartite foreign relations with our European allies rests on three legs."

Bogges took a pencil to the redundancies and then put the pencil down: let the old dip speak in his own voice. "... so the trialogue requires we consult on three fronts ... the responsibilities of the world's remaining superpower are threefold ..." It was almost soothing. Bogges skimmed comfortably on to the end. "In sum, we'd better start minding our own business."

Bogges put the letter down, got up nervously from his desk and went to his meeting.

■■■■■

We live in infinity, said Bogges to himself. It goes on forever. We aspire to eternity, outside of time or place. What prompted these reflections was the infinite tedium of the meeting Lance Morrow-Graves was conducting and the urgent desire to be someplace else. The subject today was relevance, which, so far as Bogges could see, didn't have much to do with anything.

"I want," said Morrow-Graves for the umpteenth time, "our sections to be relevant."

He seemed to be addressing the editor of Obituaries. The obit man stirred in his seat and gave Morrow-Graves his attention with a deadpan expression. The Science editor looked off into the middle distance, perhaps for the window which was not there in the cramped but brightly lit conference room. The Religion editor put his fingertips together and bowed his head. Bogges pretended to scribble a note.

"And that means we have to be more relevant all the time."

This was the last observation Morrow-Graves made that penetrated Bogges's consciousness for the next few minutes. Bogges supposed there were degrees of relevance, and irrelevance too for that matter. Still, it was hard to see how the letters page could be made more or less relevant or irrelevant since whatever people were writing in about must be what was on their minds and thus, at least to them, relevant in the first degree. He began to compose a letter by S. J. Chakravarti on the subject. Soon he was scribbling importantly and in earnest.

Sir,
I am noticing with very greatest dismay your distinguished journal's attention to things of the moment which you are saying are so much relevant. I am saying that these are passing things, and what is passing is soon not here and what is not here is gone and what is gone is not being relevant by not being here. This is logic. There is no disputing. You are telling me of what great importance are such things. What

things I am asking. I am answering. I am hearing you telling me when I am reading what you are publishing, I am now giving example of such things, that certain person is saying celebrate diversity and other certain person is saying affirm equality. Very sorry, but I must respectfully inform distinguished editors that if you are being equal you are being same and if you are being diverse you are being different. So I am writing these words on water. In that water I shall cast stone: ripples will erase these words. So, you are now seeing that these words are not relevant. Such are these things.

Distinguished journals such as your own distinguished journal should be telling me what I am wanting. This is your job. But whatever I am wanting you are not giving. I am wanting five Ws and one H. What are these things? I am telling you they are who, what, where, when, why, how? You are telling me what people are feeling what it is they are thinking that was happening when your reporter was listening. I am coming to know reporter better than happening. Why is this, I am asking. I am answering. Reporter has forgotten job for which you have hired him and I have paid cash. I am not wanting to go inside heads of people. This is people's own business. I am wanting to know what people are doing. Act is not thought—

At this point, Morrow-Graves's voice again penetrated.

"Gentlemen, our job is to get at the thinking behind the news. You might almost say that the news is thinking in action. Acts are thoughts, gentlemen. What makes those thoughts news is that they happen. When we expose the thinking, we make it relevant."

Morrow-Graves looked with satisfaction at his audience. His expression seemed to say, much like Hugo's last night, that the logic is irrefutable, what pleasure you must take in following it with me.

"What kind of changes are you proposing, Lance?" asked Science.

Morrow-Graves was delighted with the question, his glee increasing like a child swinging higher and higher.

"Change, yes, you've put your finger on it!"

"But I thought," said Religion, "that you wanted my section to emphasize the unchanging, I think you called it the immutable nature of faith."

Bogges was eager to hear Obit's thoughts. He, however, seemed unwilling to contribute.

"We could have interviews with the deceased," whispered Bogges so that only Obits could hear him. "It would be news."

Obits twitched. "The ineffable in pursuit of the unspeaking," he muttered.

"The unspeakable," Bogges corrected.

Obits opened an eye. "Oscar Wilde is also dead. I edit." Obits then lapsed back into his coma.

Morrow-Graves missed this exchange, passed on. "Yes, the immutable nature of change. That's what we're all about, what?"

"All about what?" repeated Bogges involuntarily.

"No, Eustace, change, change is what we're all about."

"Then we shouldn't change, not if change is what we're all about."

Morrow-Graves looked puzzled. Science, Religion, even Obits, were quietly sniggering.

"I'm afraid I don't quite follow, old man," said Morrow-Graves.

"I think the point that Eustace is trying to convey," said Science, "is that since change is what we're covering, to change what we're covering would imply covering something other than change."

"No, I certainly don't want you to change that."

"Of course," said Religion, "we could change how we're covering change. For example, if you gave me another page during the week, and maybe another couple of reporters, maybe a bureau in the Vatican, another in Jerusalem and, I don't know, one in the Far East somewhere, why, we would vastly extend our current abilities to cover the changing face of religion."

Morrow-Graves tried to look wistful. In fact, he was horror-struck by the idea of putting such a preposterous request to the managing editor. The very thought made him anxious. He hurried to end the meeting, which, possibly, was what Religion had had in mind.

As they filed out, Religion took Bogges by the arm.

"Have you ever noticed, Eustace, how Lance gets more English when he maunders?"

"Yes."

"I've often wondered why that is."

"The further he gets from reality, the closer he approaches a completely bogus persona."

"That must be it. I suppose you know that he's been making noises about giving you my section. You don't want it, do you?"

"Christ, no."

"Good, that's what I thought. I don't anticipate too much trouble heading him off. I just wanted to make sure that it wasn't coming from you."

"If there's anything I can do," began Bogges.

"No, I can handle Lance."

It occurred to Bogges that it might be a good idea to discuss Dr. Fall with this man. He had his feet on the ground. Bogges decided to hold off, for a while at least. He'd already talked to Abel Japrowski. He didn't want the entire editorial staff to know. Bogges ran into Japrowski outside his office. Japrowski had stopped in the middle of the corridor and was examining a document.

"Are you lurking or prowling?" asked Bogges.

Japrowski looked up just as if he'd been caught doing something he shouldn't. "Oh, good morning, Eustace. I was just reading this IPO."

"What is an IPO?" asked Bogges, who actually knew what it was but didn't feel like admitting it for some reason.

"Initial Public Offering, my innocent friend. This is the prospectus for a company that wants to sell shares to the public. The company has many competitors, no market share to speak of, and a string of losses. I'm sure it will be a great success, the sale of its stock, I mean."

"Why?"

"Because it's a pure speculation."

"Oh."

"Don't you want to know why something that's supposed to be an investment is more attractive when it's nothing more than a bet?"

"No."

"Oh. How was your date?"

"It wasn't a date, Abel. Dates are for teenagers."

"Alright, how was whatever it was that you had?"

"Fine."

Japrowski gave Bogges a wry smile. He spoke patiently, like an adult to a child. "Well, Eustace, I don't want to take up any more of your valuable time. It was great talking to you. Anytime you feel like doing more of it, you know where to find me."

"Right."

Japrowski buried his nose back in his document and moved unhurriedly away down the corridor. Bogges supposed he might have been more forthcoming with his friend. He felt distracted, oddly bemused, almost disembodied. He went back to his office. There was a note from the Managing Editor on his desk, who wanted to know when Bogges was going to begin responding to the letters by e-mail. What, he asked plaintively, is the point of having an e-mail address if you're not there to answer?

"That," said Dr. Fall, appearing suddenly, "is a very good question. What if you're not there to answer?"

"Then I won't be asked," said Bogges sourly.

"No. There you're wrong," he replied with satisfaction. "You are held responsible for certain answers whether you listen to the questions or not. And," he added grimly, "you are required to answer."

"Why?"

"Because that is the nature of things."

"What things?"

"Life. That is also the answer, by the by."

"What are you talking about?"

"I mean that you answer with your life."

Dr. Fall roared with laughter, if such a tinny laugh from the cramped voice box in that scraggly neck properly could be called a roar. Dr. Fall was dressed today in a kind of shirt with an unnecessary number of pockets, baggy khakis, and sandals with white socks. With his Van Dyke, he looked like a shrunken and deplorable Sigmund Freud on safari.

"It's a good joke, no? The very best of all jokes. The answer to the question is the question, and when you win, you lose."

"That's not fair," said Bogges.

Dr. Fall shook with merriment. "Fair, what does fair have to do with it? Rules are rules. They are not made to be fair. They are made not to be broken."

"Rules are made to be broken!" cried Bogges.

"You Americans are so childish," he sniffed.

"What does American have to do with it?"

"Nothing," replied Dr. Fall primly. "Nothing at all. It won't help you one bit."

"I don't need help."

"I think you do. Otherwise, why would you be here?"

"Why are you here?" Bogges countered.

"I come when I'm called."

"Then why won't you go when you're sent away?"

"That is one of the rules. You may summon me. You may not dismiss me."

Bogges turned his back on Dr. Fall. A stack of unread mail confronted him. He picked up a letter, saw it was a bill from Dr. Fall, and hurriedly put it down.

"Yes, you Americans are so childish," repeated Dr. Fall.

Bogges faced around. "What does being American have to do with it?"

"Nothing, Mr. Bogges, nothing. Germans are childish, French are childish, you are all childish. But, if you will permit, Americans, ah, they are so young, they are uniquely childish, childish in a way which is so, so," he pretended to hesitate, "so much their own youthful, vigorous, adolescent way. The world, Mr. Bogges, has not been so young since the Romans.

Not that you Americans are very much like the Romans. You don't have their insouciance. They were true children of nature. When they took a city, they slaughtered the men, the women, the children, they killed the dogs and the cats, they razed the buildings, they salted the earth. That was insouciance. Why, after Titus had plundered the Temple in Jerusalem, his father, the emperor Vespasian, used the treasure to finance construction of a playground."

"A playground?" asked Bogges incredulously.

"Yes, a rather grand playground. The proceeds from the destruction of Jerusalem built the Coliseum. You see, you Americans don't really know how to play. Shall I tell you when play went out of the world?"

"When you started interfering, that's my guess."

Dr. Fall looked taken aback. Perhaps he was only pretending surprise. It was impossible to tell. He shook his head.

"I never interfere. That is another rule. I encourage certain possibilities. Take a notion like alternative facts, for example. Perhaps it's the romantic in me, but I can't call that anything but playful."

"So, you're behind Trump and the White House wrecking crew. I might have guessed. And his advisors, the warlock and the witch, they belong to you?"

"Mr. Bogges, the entire point of humans is to portray in miniature the infinitely playful variety of being. However, professional ethics prevent me from commenting on who is and who is not a patient. You may rest assured that our confidentiality will never be breached by me."

Dr. Fall waited for Bogges to respond, perhaps with a confession that he'd spoken to Marina and Japrowski. Bogges remained silent. After the briefest pause, Dr. Fall spoke as though no response had been expected.

"All men need encouragement. Or, perhaps, all men require temptation. They are essentially the same."

Bogges gave him a discouraging look. It did not affect Dr. Fall in the least. He continued musing as though Bogges wasn't there.

"I can resist anything except temptation, said a wise man. He spoke for us all. That is why the great temptation had to be invented; another rule,

you'll observe. The heavenly paradise, I mean, THE HEAVENLY PARA-
DISE. It took time to sink in, the glorious implications, but once it did,
who could resist?"

Dr. Fall looked up from his folded hands with a modest expression, as if
he had himself invented this marvelous device but didn't like to boast. The
little man's presumption was insufferable.

"If you're trying to convince me that heaven is a fiction, you're wasting
your breath," said Bogges.

"Wouldn't you like to know what heaven is," asked Dr. Fall temptingly.

"I bet your version is hell."

"Touché, Mr. Bogges, touché."

"Will you stop using French?"

"Of course, my dear fellow, of course, infinite apologies."

Dr. Fall sounded exactly like Morrow-Graves pretending to be English.
Not that the falsity of his regret needed emphasis. Bogges wondered what
he had meant by infinite apologies. It sounded menacing. Dr. Fall resumed
his psychiatric manner.

"You will recall that we were discussing money when we last met. It was
understood from its invention that money represented all earthly desires
or at least their potential fulfillment. To the unimaginative, money was infinite potential. It was as far as their poor imaginations, their impoverished
faculties, would take them. The better sort were left unsatisfied. This could
not be allowed. Life must be satisfactory, it was felt. The solution was to
take away the here and now, something, you will observe, money emphatically does not. But take away life, as it were, and life will prove adequate
even to the imaginatively gifted. It had been attempted before. Siddhartha,
a near contemporary of that other dreamer, Sadyattes, had had some success. But his methods were too demanding. Still, one admires a man who
insists that the only desirable desire is the elimination of desire. He showed
a sense of humor. There was an element of playfulness which suggested that
a joke was involved. However, eliminate the butt of the joke, as Siddhartha
recommended, and who would be left to laugh? It wouldn't do. The Jews
were a serious people. They were chosen. One of their number discovered

that he had only to eliminate the joke and keep the butt. This, you will admit, was elegant. Naturally, the kingdom of heaven did not have the immediate appeal of money. Money had caught on right away, an instant hit. Heaven, on the other hand, takes a while to grow on you. It helps if life appears to be unsatisfactory. In fact, it's required. By the end of the fourth century of the Common Era all the requirements had been met. And so, in 390 CE the Emperor of Rome humbled himself before the Bishop of Milan. On that day, the Classical Era ended and play went out of the world."

"That's ludicrous," said Bogges.

"Yes, it is, isn't it? However, I'm afraid that's precisely what happened."

"That's not what I meant," said Bogges with irritation. "I meant that it's ludicrous to assert that the Classical Era ended at one point in time and that play went out of the world."

"Nevertheless, the man with the greatest freedom chose to give up his freedom on account of an empty threat and for a nonexistent reward, and so play went out like a light. Thus, the Dark Ages."

"And why was that?"

"Because of a rape in Thessalonika."

"Oh God, another rape."

"Not God—man, in fact, a homosexual rape. The plebs of Thessalonika were addicted to chariot races. When the star charioteer was arrested for the rape, they turned on the garrison, murdered the commander, mutilated the corpse, and dragged the remains through the streets. The news reached Emperor Theodosius in Milan. He devised a most royal punishment, a model of imperial insouciance. He directed the garrison to allow the citizens of Thessalonika to enter the hippodrome and enjoy their innocent entertainments. Once inside, the gates were to be locked, and every man, woman, and child was to be slain. The killing went on for hours. They were mowed down like ears of corn. Among the myriad poignant scenes, one in particular stands out in memory. A wealthy citizen, a father, offered himself and all his riches if the soldiers would only let his two sons go free. The soldiers, in a playful mood, replied that they would free one of the boys and the father must quickly choose which it was to be. The poor man looked longingly at one, then the other. Never had the two boys seemed so dear, so worthy of love, so deserving of life, so irreplaceable. To choose between them was a horror, not to choose, a blasphemy. The soldiers grew tired of the father's indecision and slew them both. Fifteen thousand died that day. One hopes the father was among that number. However, knowing something about Gothic humor, I suspect the soldiers permitted the father to live."

"Don't you know for certain?" interrupted Bogges.

"Of course."

"Well?"

"Stories," said Dr. Fall conversationally, "are more effective if they're left open-ended. It encourages a sense of wonder, don't you think? Where would you be if I answered all your questions? It's so much more tempting to have something to look forward to. This was Theodosius's view of the matter. He also wanted something to look forward to, in his case, the kingdom of heaven. It was a measure of the unsatisfactory state of the Roman Empire, what was left of it, that even its emperor was dissatisfied with the here and now. Thus, the Bishop of Milan, one Ambrose, an admirer of virgins, orthodoxy, and the hereafter, felt able to threaten Theodosius with excommunication if he would not do penance for the massacre of Thessalonika. Ambrose threatened that Theodosius would not get what he, Ambrose, didn't have to give unless Theodosius gave up what he, Theodosius, did have.

"Of course, even a bishop as alive to his own importance as Ambrose wouldn't dare challenge the emperor without some outside aid. Providentially, Ambrose had had a dream. Ambrose dreamt that he was saying Mass, that Theodosius entered the cathedral and that he, Ambrose, was instantly rendered powerless to offer the bread and wine to the communicants. At this time, August 22, 390 CE, a comet appeared which illuminated the heavens until September 17. Ambrose was persuaded that the sole purpose of this celestial phenomenon was to signal the approval of the three-in-one god and confirm him in his course. Ambrose retired to the country and composed a letter to Theodosius. This miserable rhapsody, as the historian of Rome's decline called it, struck two notes. Ambrose himself would sin if he didn't insist on Theodosius asking forgiveness; moreover, there was royal precedent: King David had once asked forgiveness for murder. Now, in the glory days of the empire, this sniveling lèse-majesté would have earned Ambrose a well-deserved sentence of torture and death. But Ambrose knew his man. Even so, it took Theodosius some weeks to steel himself. But the day came when the emperor of Britain, Gaul, and Spain, of Egypt and North Africa, of Italy and the Alps, the Balkans and Greece, the islands of the Mediterranean and the Aegean, all Asia Minor from the coasts of Turkey, Lebanon, and Palestine to the western border of Persia, the emperor of Rome and of Constantinople, presented himself before the doors of the cathedral of Milan. There waiting for him, beard and mustache meeting in a circle around his mouth like an O of delight, and his great sheep's eyes hiding the light of the wolf beneath, dressed in a simple linen tunic and a heavy brown cloak, Ambrose welcomed the penitent. Theodosius wore a robe of Tyrian purple embroidered with golden crosses over a snowy tunic girt with a crimson sash. His legs and feet were attired in purple hose and crimson slippers. He entered and walked alone down the nave. At the farther end, he passed under a lofty arch to the transept. In the center stood the altar, a marble slab supported on pillars. The onlookers, I mean the worshippers, a great crowd eager to take part in this edifying scene, now gave a gasp of astonishment which echoed up and down the hollow length of the basilica. For Theodosius cast off the purple before sinking to his knees. Only Ambrose smiled. Only Ambrose understood that henceforth, no man should be free."

"And what, may I ask, is the point of this endless rant?" said Bogges.

"I thought you might like to know how life came to be so circumscribed."

"That's your view."

"Surely, it's the view of any sensible man." Dr. Fall gestured at Bogges's tiny, airless, cluttered office. "This, I suppose, represents freedom?"

Bogges sighed. There seemed no reply. Dr. Fall, however, had plenty to say.

"The truth shall set you free, Mr. Bogges. And the truth is that you would not be where you are if Theodosius had not cast off the purple and humiliated himself before a powerless monk in a sackcloth."

Bogges was suddenly inspired.

"You remind me of a girl I took on a picnic years ago," he said. "She picked up a twig from the ground and moved it from one side of her cup to the other. Then she told me very solemnly that she had changed the universe."

"That would be Janet Rouse." Dr. Fall didn't miss a beat. "She wished to come under my care. I considered taking her on but decided against. I believe you arrived at the same conclusion."

This was unsettling, not because Dr. Fall knew the name of the girl Bogges had referred to. It was the fact that Dr. Fall had evidently found Janet as tiresome as he, Bogges, had found her. There was no escaping a sense of fellow feeling.

"Of course, one might have forgiven Theodosius if he had bowed before mankind's true savior. However, that birth was still eleven hundred years off."

"Who is that?" asked Bogges in a weak voice.

"Why, it's just li'l ole me."

Sally Benton sashayed into the room. Dr. Fall had vanished.

"What is that terrible odor, Eustace?"

There was a mephitic stink, rotting fish mixed with heated pencil shavings and burning brake pads.

"I don't believe the cleaning staff have been in here in a month of Sundays. It's downright unsanitary," she said.

Sally looked disapprovingly at the mess. She waved a small, plump hand. The nails were tipped blood red. A wisp of blond hair had escaped the knot at the back of her head. The office now also reeked of Southern femininity.

"Devil farts," muttered Bogges.

"What was that you said?"

"Nothing. I don't smell nothing. I mean anything."

The smell was dissipating. There was only the faintest reek.

"What are you doing here, Sally?"

"Just paying a call on my first day."

"Oh. Yes. Nice of you to stop by. How are things going so far?"

"Well, JT has introduced me to practically everyone. I do think that Lance Morrow-Graves is just darling. And I'm going to have lunch with Mr. Thersites."

Thersites was the executive editor. Bogges, except at office parties, had never dined with Thersites. It had never occurred to him that having lunch alone with Thersites would be a good idea, from the point of view of calculation, or pleasurable, from the point of view of company. Bogges examined his feelings about keeping company with Thersites and found that they hadn't changed.

"That should be nice," he said.

"I'm just thrilled to death."

This struck a poignant note. Bogges recollected that thrilled was the verb Sally used to refer to intimate physical acts. He thought, by a logical extension, about food.

"It's almost lunchtime," he said. "I'm sorry you can't join me."

"Why, you sweet thing."

The invitation had cost him nothing; Bogges congratulated himself. He picked up the Chakravarti letter he'd composed and decided it needed work. He didn't think Sally would take the hint.

"I already have the subject for my first column," she said brightly.

Bogges put the letter face down on his knee. "I thought you were going to review books," he said.

"Oh, I am. But books are just an excuse for me to air my opinions. JT says that my mind is an infallible gloss on the zeitgeist. He respects me for my intellect, Eustace."

Bogges chose to overlook this reprimand. "So what are you going to write about?" He asked this with genuine curiosity.

Sally drew herself up and composed her features. "The battle of the sexes is over. Men and women can both declare victory. The playing field is leveled. Everyone can now market their own brand in free and open competition. Joy is the mission statement for modern relationships."

"That is very provoking," said Bogges.

Sally arched her back, swung her hips. "I aim to be provocative. JT says he's gonna syndicate me."

"That's because he's a pimp." Bogges was instantly sorry he'd spoken. Sally swelled an angry pink, matching her dress.

"If you'd listened to me, you would have been managing editor by now. But no, getting ahead was beneath you." The accent was acid. "Let me tell you, Eustace Bogges, that making something of yourself in this world takes guts. JT has the kind of guts you never even imagined."

"You have a point."

The habits of married life do not easily die. Bogges felt abashed. He hadn't meant to sound sarcastic when he said that Sally had a point.

"Yes, I do. But I don't believe for a moment that you understand what the point is. I used to think you understood about everything. Then I thought you could understand when you wanted to. Then I finally realized that you didn't want to any more."

Bogges decided that he preferred Dr. Fall's company to Sally's. This set off another train of thought. If marriage was hell and divorce did not provide relief, what was there to look forward to? Dr. Fall was apparently going to offer an answer. Bogges wondered if it would be good for him to know. That's what Sally had said years ago when she had told him she was having an affair: it was good for him to know. Of course, it hadn't felt that way at the time. She'd seemed surprised when he told her to get out. She wasn't ready to make that commitment. You're not making a commitment, he'd said, you're breaking one. Why would I want to do that, she'd asked. He had walked out at that point. He thought he might do it again. He heaved himself up and left.

The wait for the elevator was long. Since most of Bogges's colleagues took the stairs—as a health measure, not just because they were in a hurry—the delay could only mean that the maintenance crew were using it. Or not using it. They had a key that took the elevator out of service. In principle, this was for work associated with the upkeep of the building. In practice, they tended to shut the elevator down for no apparent reason, usually when it was most wanted. Perhaps it was a form of preventive maintenance: the elevator can't break down if it's not being used. When the elevator doors did finally open, Bogges's face was mottled. A man in overalls with almost no chin turned off the elevator and stepped out. His hands were unusually large, more like tools then hands, depending from long sinewy arms. He waved a prehensile appendage at Bogges, and one side of his mouth twitched open.

"Out of service."

Bogges pretended not to hear. He marched in and punched lobby. Nothing happened except that the workman repeated, using more of his mouth, that the elevator was out of service. He spoke louder and in a somewhat threatening tone. Bogges spotted the key in the control panel at about the same moment the workman began searching his pocket. Bogges was quicker. When he reached the lobby, he pocketed the key for safekeeping.

Bogges headed for Marina's hut changed his mind when he came in sight of it. To see Marina would mean discussing Dr. Fall's latest visit. Marina, as a woman, would expect Bogges, as a friend, to tell her everything that had happened to him since she had last seen him, even if it was only last night. This, in Bogges's view, is a difference between men and women: men are content to express companionship with anything that might come to mind; women require the latest news of you. Bogges ate at a steakhouse. On his way out, he saw Sally, JT, and Thersites at a distance. They were at what appeared to be the best table having what appeared to be the best time. Several workmen were in the lobby when he returned to the paper. The lobby was undergoing renovations. The workmen were not helping with this project. They seemed to be loitering. One was the workman Bogges had encountered in the elevator. It was clear he was waiting for him. Bogges thought the others were probably helping him do that. He was sorry he hadn't made up the letters page before lunch. He thought longingly of the rear entrance. It had been sealed off more than two decades ago when the paper had moved its printing operations to the suburbs. This was at the time when the newsroom had become computerized. The two events were related: something else to hold against computers. Calling in a fire alarm struck Bogges as overly dramatic. Relinquishing the key before he had a copy made was out of the question. He shifted to and fro before the entrance, coming heavily down on one leg then the other in an effort to aid thought. The pounding stimulated his bladder. This, in turn, gave him an idea. He went around the corner to the city's last remaining phone booth, which was more like a urinal stall than a booth, called the paper's main number, and asked to be connected to the security guard in the lobby.

"Thish ish Mishter Thershites," said Bogges when he'd gotten him.

"Yes, sir."

"Theresh a flood in the exshecutive men'sh room on the ninth floor. Shend up everyone you've got."

"Right away, sir!"

This was not at all how Thersites sounded. But the guard couldn't be expected to know this because he had never heard Thersites speak. Bogges gave it a minute before strolling into the empty lobby. He took a moment to wish the guard a good afternoon before going up to his office.

CHAPTER SEVEN

The workman was again waiting, or still waiting, in the lobby next morning. Bogges wished he'd had a chance to try the new key before giving up the old one. He solved this problem by offering the copy. The workman snatched it with a grimace.

"You had no cause to go and do that," he said.

"I think you've got that wrong," replied Bogges pleasantly.

"You think so?"

"I'm sure of it. The elevator is there for my convenience."

"I got work to do here, mister."

This was said with the contempt that people who earn their livings standing up sometimes have for people who earn their livings sitting down.

"We all bear that cross, brother," said Bogges leaving quickly by the elevator before the workman could respond. He found Jonah Thomas waiting for him outside his office.

"Your door's locked," said JT in greeting.

"Locks are for honest men," said Bogges. "I congratulate you."

"What the hell does that mean?"

"A thief would not be stopped by a lock," explained Bogges.

"Cut the crap, Eustace. I got a call from a source in the White House. They're interested in some guy named S. J. Chakravarti; only, they can't find him."

Bogges hardly fumbled with his keys at all while unlocking the door.

"Who," he said over his shoulder, "is Chakravarti?"

"How the hell should I know? You tell me—you printed his letter."

"I print a lot of letters. I don't know most of the correspondents."

By now, Bogges had the door open. Thomas followed him into the office.

"I want you to look in your files so that I can pass on this guy's address."

Thomas looked uncomfortable. While not strictly a source, people who wrote letters to the paper had some right to privacy. The paper didn't give out its readers' home addresses, unless it was selling its subscription list to another corporation. In other words, it wasn't ethical to betray readers' privacy individually.

"Who wants to know?" said Bogges.

"You know I can't reveal a source," said Thomas.

"Why does the White House want to talk to this Chakravarti; do I have the name right?"

Thomas didn't want to give away even this much. He agreed that that was the name.

"But why are they interested in him?" repeated Bogges.

Thomas struggled with himself. "They think," he said with an effort, "that there's something in this mind-your-own-business business. They want to talk to him about it, find out what he means."

Bogges gaped. Then he laughed. "They need a consultant to advise them on how to mind their own business!"

Thomas's features resumed their customary expression of impatience. "I think they see this as a way to explain their foreign policy."

"I can't reveal a reader's address."

"Stop fooling around, Eustace. This is important."

Bogges smiled. "No, really, it's not."

Thomas looked dumbfounded. "Christ, you're really from another world. This is the White House, for Christ's sake. This Chakravarti character may define the first year of the administration. Don't you see that? Don't you think you have some obligation to the future?"

"No more than I do to the past," said Bogges automatically.

Thomas was growing desperate. "This is a scoop, you damn fool."

Bogges was still enough of a newsman to respond to the magic word.

"I'll tell you what," he said. "I'll contact this Chakravarti character and see if he wants to talk to your source in the White House."

Thomas looked dissatisfied. However, he couldn't see a way of eliminating Bogges from the equation.

"When will I hear from you?"

"When I hear from Chakravarti."

When he was alone, Bogges discovered that he felt lighthearted. He began humming an old song to himself: "If You Got the Money Honey, I Got the Time." After a moment, he started singing the words out loud. Then he bent at the waist and stiffly dangled an arm like the trunk of an aged elephant in front of his nose. Ponderously he shuffled and swayed, rotating his shoulders and waggling his hips. He added an up and down motion, bending first at one knee then at the other. He careered around his office, voice rising in rapturous song: "If you've got the money honey, I've got the tiiiime ..." Round and round he swept, pirouetting on his hoofs and dangling his trunk, trumpeting his joy to the crash of toppling furniture and books and the rustling collapse of piles of unread mail. His trance was broken by the ringing telephone, which had been knocked to the floor. He sank to his knees to pick up the receiver and then tried to maneuver his rump onto the floor with the aid of the other hand. This didn't work, and he spent the entirety of the conversation in the suppliant position.

"They found someone named Chakravarti, but apparently he's not the right one," said Thomas's voice.

"I know." Bogges spoke breathlessly, sounding, perhaps, conspiratorial.

"How do you know that?"

"I've just been in contact with him."

"How do you know it's the right one?"

Bogges chose not to answer. "Who were they talking to?"

"Some guy in Arlington who runs a grocery. He said he was an honest man who minds his own business. So the White House thought they had the right guy. But it turns out that he's almost illiterate and an illegal. He doesn't write letters to the editor."

"What's going to happen to him?"

"How the hell should I know? Deport him, I guess."

Reluctantly, for Bogges had ideas about the hard working underclass, he concentrated on the matter at hand. "He's willing to talk to your guy at the White House, under certain conditions."

"What are they?"

"He's very protective of his privacy. He doesn't want to become a public figure. But he's patriotic, up to a point. He'll take a call from your friend at my house."

"I'll be there to monitor."

"No, you won't. He was very definite, no strangers. He feels he knows me."

"You'll file the story."

"Well, Thomas, I'll have to ask Mr. Chakravarti about that. Of course, I could write something about whatever the source in the White House says."

"Don't use the source's name." Thomas sounded panicked.

"Why don't you tell me who this source of yours is?"

Thomas hesitated. "Bannon and Conway," he pronounced.

Bogges laughed and didn't stop laughing while he instructed Thomas at what time to have the White House call. The phone rang again a few minutes later.

"Eustace, this is Morrow-Graves. Mr. Thersites is here in my office. Apparently there's a flood of some kind on the executive floor and he'd like to talk to you."

A commanding voice took the phone. "Bogges, I understand you don't have a computer at home. How are you going to file that story tonight?"

"I'll phone it in."

"You mean you'll dictate it?"

"Certainly."

"It's been fifteen years since anyone did that."

"More's the pity."

The executive editor hung up. This did nothing to suppress Bogge's spirits. Later, while he was preparing his page, he became curious about the flood on the executive floor. When the elevator didn't come, he walked up the two flights. Upstairs, the elevator was waiting, out of service, water lapping at its open doors. Water was also eddying down the length of the hall. The Persian runner which led from the walnut-paneled lobby to the offices of Thersites and the publisher had turned a deeper, marine blue. The lobby was deserted, and the walls were beaded with the damp. Bogges thought he could already detect signs of warping. Rough voices could be heard from the direction of the men's room discussing wrenches, shut-off valves, water mains. Bogges stood awhile in thought. Then he went back downstairs.

■■■■■

His home phone rang at precisely 7:02 p.m.

"This is the White House calling for Mr. Chakravarti."

"I'll see if he's available. Who shall I say is calling?"

There was the slightest pause. "The president is holding."

Bogges put the phone down and mumbled at his martini. Then he picked up the phone again. "Put him on. Mr. Chakravarti will be right there."

"I can't make the connection until Mr. Chakravarti is on the line."

This was nonsense. Bogges hung up. The phone started ringing before Bogges had time to reach for his drink. He let it ring until he had drunk. The petulant New York tones on the other end of the line were familiar, like hearing from a distasteful family connection.

"I love that, really love that, most people, so sad, can't negotiate, don't know how to win, clueless. You, you were negotiating my phone call, the president's phone call, beautiful, so beautiful, wanna come work for me?"

Bogges assumed the Chakravarti persona. "White House or business enterprise, O Ruler of the World?"

"Well, money's better in the organization. Talk to my kid, OK? But we're gonna make something of this, trust me, we're really gonna make something of all these connections, for all of us, we the people. Who'd a thought there'd be all these connections. It's complicated, but it's very very good."

"Your business, Sahib, is business of the people, minding your own business you are minding business of the people."

"That's what I've been saying, I make a statement, everyone goes crazy, nuts. Then, what I predict, it happens, sometimes a period of time, but it happens, over and over. What's good for my business is good for the people's business. I'm a very instinctual person. There are people who know me, big, important people, they understand me, they get it. Many many things they turn out to be right. My instincts they turn out to be right. You know what we're gonna do? I'm gonna mind my own business right here in the White House. I'm gonna make a speech tomorrow, from the Oval Office, a beautiful speech, everyone's gonna love it."

"O Pathfinder of the Forward Going Way, minding your own business is most assuredly the foundation of prosperity and health."

"What can you say? I've been saying it for a long time. See how sick poor people are, so sad, kind of like the chicken and the egg, which came first, good question. But, if we make poor people rich, not as rich as me, but rich, plenty of money, I bet they feel better in a hurry, right away. Obamacare finished, no one wants it. Trumpcare, makes everyone rich, everyone healthy. Mind your own business. Even the fake news media can understand. If they mind their own business they'll understand. If they don't, enemies of the people. The people want to mind their own business. That's why they voted for me, record numbers. They know I mind my own business. When America starts minding its own business we'll be so great again. I'll make American great again by making everyone mind their own business. I didn't know it was so easy. Lots of things people say I don't know. It doesn't matter. I know more than the experts, more than the generals. I see possibilities, many many possibilities."

"Yes, Sahib, not knowing means all is possible, like infinity, very most many possibilities."

"Yeah, infinite possibilities. That's how I do business, plenty of credit when I promise infinite possibilities."

"I am asking question."

"OK."

"Warlock and witch on your staff, will they be helping make America mind its own business?"

"Who leaked that? Confidential personnel matters, I choose the greatest, the best, we need an investigation, I'm ordering an investigation, now!"

The president hung up, and Bogges reached for his drink. He finished his martini, called the National Desk, and began dictating.

"A source close to the president, no, make that a source with intimate knowledge of the president's thinking said today that the White House is preparing to launch a new, make that a major new, policy initiative which is being viewed as President Trump's legacy to history, stop. The initiative comma which is to be called Mind Your Own Business comma is said to emphasize personal responsibility and will be promoted through the president's powers of moral suasion stop. Paragraph.

"While still vague in detail comma the broad outline has prompted some critics to wonder why the president is injecting, no, I can't say that, oh, the hell with it, why the president is injecting himself into the middle of what is potentially a serious controversy. Scratch that, that made no sense at all. Read me the beginning of the graph. OK. While vague in detail comma the broad outline has prompted skeptics to wonder what business it is of the president's stop. One observer comma S.J. Chakravarti comma that's capital C-h-a-k-r-a-v-a-r-t-i, suggested that if the president were really serious about minding his own business comma the least he could do would be to shut up stop. Yes, that's what he said. Well, fine, have the night people call around for comment. Yes, I'll give you a last graf, you can fill in the middle with whatever you guys come up with. While alive to the controversial aspect of Mind Your Own Business comma the White House source affirmed that comma quote We will make the poor rich end quote."

▪▪▪▪▪

There was a note from Thersites on Bogges's desk next morning, what was called in his early newspaper days a herogram.

"Great story, we scooped everybody. What are you doing for me today?"

"Ahem."

Morrow-Graves stood outside the door. He'd contorted his body so that only his head was visible, the remainder of his long trunk and limbs twisted out of sight somewhere in the hall. It, he, looked extremely uncomfortable.

"Mr. Thersites has asked me to make up your page while you're working on the Chakravarti profile," he said.

Bogges wondered if the moment had come to resign. It was too bad that his pension was still five years away from being completely funded. He supposed he could sell his house in Georgetown and move to a condominium in, no, not Florida. Bogges didn't think Arizona would do either.

"This is news to me, Lance."

Morrow-Graves sighed. The word news appeared to depress him.

"It was JT's idea," he said. "Mr. Thersites agreed that it was our duty to profile the man behind Mind Your Own Business. You seem to be the only one he'll talk to, Eustace."

This was said so wistfully that, if it had been in Bogges's power, he would have given Morrow-Graves the interview. This, on consideration, made sense.

"I don't think I'm up to it, Lance."

Morrow-Graves smiled bravely. "I would say that your performance last night showed that it's well within your powers."

"I think you could do a better job."

Morrow-Graves untwisted his body and entered Bogges's office. "That is very kind of you, old chap."

Bogges gritted his teeth. "Chakravarti trusts me. If I asked him for an interview, he might think I was using him. I can't betray his trust. But if I asked him to talk to somebody I trusted, I wouldn't be betraying his trust. At least, not in the same way."

"Yes, I quite see that."

"So you'll do it?"

"Well ..." Morrow-Graves's body had begun contorting again. "Well, if you really think it would be best, of course, I would be delighted to help."

"Thanks, Lance."

"Just let me know when Mr. Chakravarti, is, er, available."

"After dark, I mean tonight, say 9:00 at my house."

"Should I bring a tape recorder?"

"Absolutely not, it would scare him right off. Notebook and pen, no, pencil, that's best."

Morrow-Graves and Bogges had each risen in the other's estimation. They looked at each other with approval and some affection.

"Until tonight, then," said Morrow-Graves.

"Right."

When he was alone, he called Marina.

"What was the name of that priest you wanted me to talk to?"

"Father Roche. I'm glad you've decided to see him. I read your story today in the paper. I'm so proud of you, Eustace, the front page and the first story too."

"The lead story," said Bogges without enthusiasm.

Marina caught the tone. "What's wrong? Something's happened. You've seen Dr. Fall again, haven't you?"

"No, I mean, yes."

"Are you alright?"

"It's a little complicated."

"Father Roche will help you sort it out. It won't be complicated to him."

Marina gave Bogges Father Roche's number and, after he had promised to see her soon, hung up. He didn't call the priest right away but sat with his hand on the phone thinking about what he would say. When he thought he'd got it right, he punched the number. A voice identified itself as Father Roche. It was a dry voice, without a hint of a French accent except perhaps that its very dryness might be French. Father Roche spoke quietly. He sounded weary and also skeptical.

"This is Eustace Bogges. One of your parishioners, Marina Niemalle, suggested I call you."

"Yes?"

"I would like to consult you about certain, ah, problems that have arisen."

"What are these problems?"

"I suppose you'd call them spiritual problems."

"I call most problems spiritual problems."

This seemed glib. Bogges decided to pursue it. "Do you think third-degree burns or bladder cancer are spiritual problems?"

"Is that what you called to ask me?"

"No."

After this there was a pause. Bogges could feel the priest waiting on the other end of the line. He didn't seem to be waiting patiently or impatiently. It was more like a vacuum. In the vacuum, Bogges thought that, from a certain point of view, burns and cancer could be seen as spiritual problems, not that they didn't remain problems in other ways too. The conversation wasn't going the way he'd expected.

"I'm calling you because I think I'm being visited by the Devil, and because of certain coincidences."

There was another pause. "Are you saying that you think you are possessed?"

"No. I mean, technically, you might say that, but I don't feel possessed."

"What is it precisely you would like me to do?"

Bogges was sorry he'd called. He thought about hanging up, didn't.

"I'd like to come talk to you."

"Unfortunately, I am leaving tomorrow for New Guinea."

"When will you be back?"

"In two weeks."

"Perhaps you could suggest someone else I might talk to?"

Another pause. "No, I can't think of anyone else."

"Well, I'll call you when you get back."

"As you wish."

■■■■■

In the event, the president did not make a speech. A series of tweets beginning late morning while he was on his way to a golf course served to convey his thoughts.

"Time America went back to minding its own business. Minders going into every Department. Courts Congress Corporations should follow."

"Anybody who minds his own business can get rich. Just watch my White House."

"S. J. Chakravarti, great American, will get Nobel Prize. He knows how to mind his own business."

An immediate effect of the president's policy was that the White House press corps were forbidden ever again to ask questions at the daily briefing.

"The news is the announcements I make," said the press secretary. "When you write down what I announce, you are covering the news. If it's too much trouble to write down what I say," she added maliciously, "after I read the daily announcements, printed copies will be made available."

Bogges considered how he might disguise himself as Mr. Chakravarti for the evening's interview with Morrow-Graves. A flowing nightgown left over from the Sally Benton regime would be suitably exotic lending, he felt, an oriental cast to his appearance. He might darken his face with shoe polish. He wondered if this notion had been put into his head by Dr. Fall, realized it certainly had, and instantly dismissed it. Bogges recollected vaguely a voluminous hairnet Sally had left behind, then more vividly that said hairnet had been worn on those nights when intimate physical acts were not welcome. It wasn't much of a disguise perhaps, but it would do for Morrow-Graves, who only saw what he expected to see. He expected to see Mr. Chakravarti and that, in addition to the dimmest of lighting, was who he would see.

It was an exotic figure that answered Morrow-Graves's knock that night. Morrow-Graves wore a surprised expression. "Ah, ah, you are, ah, Mr. Chakravarti?"

"This is being most precisely the case."

"Where is Eustace?"

"He is not available because he is not being here due to other obligations he must be attending to. Please to make yourself at home by coming in."

Morrow-Graves sat himself down in the indicated chair under the front parlor's single illuminated floor lamp and peered into the gloom. "May I ask why you wear a veil?"

"I honor the God who is present but not seen by wearing a veil."

"You look somehow familiar. Have we met before?"

"That is because I am looking so much like myself. You are perhaps recognizing other people you are knowing who look very much like themselves. You are now seeing the resemblance."

"Yes, perhaps that's it. Now," he said, banishing a look of puzzlement, "how does it feel to have the President of the United States announce you deserve the Nobel Prize?"

"The President is offering what he is not having to give. He is being a most generous man."

Morrow-Graves looked up from the notebook in which he'd been scribbling. "So you're an admirer of the president?"

"I am not knowing him."

"You only admire people you know?"

"I am knowing both kinds."

"Which kind is the President?"

"I am not knowing."

Morrow-Graves gave this up. "What gave you the idea of minding your own business?" he asked.

"I am not calling it idea."

"How would you describe it then?"

Chakravarti spread his arms with palms out. "I am calling it my pet. It is being a jewel and a gem, so big and yet so small. I am turning it over and over, I am examining it from every angle, I am admiring its many facets. See how it is catching the light, how it is shattering all things when we are viewing one way and, viewing another way, how all things are reassembling into seamless and wholesome oneness. There is no thing it is not penetrating and, behold, it is leaving no mark. Everything is being transformed, and no thing is being changed. It is"—his voice dropped to a whisper—"the uncleft fundament on which are resting all things."

"Quite so," said Morrow-Graves skeptically.

"I am asking question," said Chakravarti.

"Fire away, old chap."

"What is it that nature did, is doing, will do?"

"Well, when you put it that way, I'm not quite sure."

Chakravarti roared, "Nature minds no business but her own business!"

"I see," replied Morrow-Graves. "You're talking about a kind of ethics based on natural law, is that right?"

"If you are insisting."

"Could you tell me how something like love thy neighbor fits into your system?"

"I am most especially loving neighbor who minds own business."

Morrow-Graves laughed. "I too would love to have neighbors like that. I can see that you have given this a lot of thought. I think I have enough theory, if you know what I mean. Perhaps we could turn to the personal side for a moment."

"What is personal side?"

"Well, you know, where are you from, what do you do, who are you?"

"I am that I am," said Chakravarti humbly.

Morrow-Graves wrote this down. "And what do you do for a living?"

"I am facilitator of that which is being conveyed."

"Ah, something to do with computers. Tell me about your background."

"I am like every man: I come from where I've been."

'Very mysterious, Mr. Chakravarti." Morrow-Graves again assumed a skeptical expression, investigative reporter relentlessly seeking truth. "And where precisely is it that you've been?"

"Many places. Would you like me to describe your place of work, for example, and paradigm of same?"

Morrow-Graves allowed a look of triumph to cross his features. "Come now, Mr. Chakravarti, many people have had occasion to visit the newsroom."

"I am not talking about newsroom which, as you are correctly pointing out, many people have had pleasure of visiting. I am talking about private quarters of your own self."

Morrow-Graves spoke with infinite condescension: "Be my guest."

Bogges began to describe Morrow-Graves's office, desk facing the door so that Morrow-Graves might never be surprised, the nine reference books, the knick-knacks, native work in straw and wicker, china figurines from France, college and university diplomas, the frequently and personally emptied wastebasket lined with a supermarket shopping bag, each and everything in its place. Morrow-Graves had passed from skepticism to triumph to condescension to awed disbelief. The range of emotions had been exhausting. He looked drawn.

"I say, old man, this is fantastic. Someone must have told you all this."

"I am not needing to be told. I am knowing."

"But how?"

"I am minding my own business."

Morrow-Graves took a deep breath. "Do you mean to say that you know all this because of some kind of intuition?"

"Very much not! I am knowing this because I am seeing this."

'And you've seen this because you mind your own business?"

"Very much yes!"

"I never would have believed it if I hadn't heard it myself." Morrow-Graves was talking to himself. He looked up at Bogges and asked in a mild and self-deprecatory tone, "Tell me, Mr. Chakravarti, what is going to happen if everyone starts minding their own business?"

"I am not knowing for sure, exactly. Maybe we will be having earthly paradise, maybe nothing will change, maybe these are same things."

Morrow-Graves looked around at Bogges's bilious green parlor, the overflowing mail table, the bar cart, the shabby carpet, the worn furniture. Morrow-Graves looked, and it was apparent that some upheaval of the spirit was taking place. His gaze had the awestruck regard of a child's. He turned this gaze on Bogges.

"Do you know, Mr. Chakravarti, I feel as though I'm seeing for the first time. Everything seems so fresh, so alive, so full of significance. Everything, as you say, has been transformed, and yet nothing is changed. Why, you yourself, I admit when I first saw you, not that I really could see, when I first laid eyes on you I thought you looked like, well, like a joke. But now I see that the way you look is the way you must look, just as this chair must have four legs and the bar cart must have wheels and the telephone must have a mouthpiece, and everything must be the way it is because, well, that is what is."

"Mind your own business," said Bogges, resuming, for a moment, his own voice.

"Yes," said Morrow-Graves as if in a dream, "yes, that's what I'm doing, I'm minding my own business. What a gay, giddy feeling."

Morrow-Graves fell silent. He began staring at his hand, twisting it this way and that and then holding it out at arm's length, transfixed by the miraculous fact of his own five digits. Bogges watched this performance with an equal degree of wonder. He got up and went over to take the hand in his in an effort to break the trance. He shook it. Morrow-Graves let out a sigh and slowly stood up.

'Extraordinary," he murmured. Then he seemed to come back to himself. "Is there a number where I can reach you if I have any follow-up questions?"

"This is not being possible since I am already going out of town."

"Where can I reach you while you're away?"

"Not possible. Perhaps, you are telling boss I will be in contact."

Morrow-Graves looked happy with this solution. "That is very kind of you," he said. "Thank you again and goodnight. Please, I'll see myself out."

Morrow-Graves was part way out when he was engaged in conversation on the doorstep. Bogges could hear only one side:

"No, Mr. Bogges is not here. Yes, as a matter of fact, his friend Mr. Chakravarti is. Well, I suppose you might. Goodnight."

Morrow-Graves passed from sight, and Dr. Fall shut the door behind himself. He was wearing a long, white silk shirt with a Nehru collar and white cotton pants that bulged at the hips and tapered to fit snugly around the ankles. Bogges supposed they were jodhpurs. His bare feet were shod in some kind of sandals. Bogges was interested to note that they were indeed feet.

"So other people can see you too," said Bogges.

Dr. Fall proceeded to the bar and spoke with his back to Bogges while mixing a drink. "Why shouldn't they be able to see me?"

Bogges chose not to answer. "I want to take a shower. Would you please go away?"

"You'll have time for that later. Here, let me give you a martini."

He mixed another drink and brought it over. Bogges sat down, and Dr. Fall placed himself on the carpet in front of Bogges's chair. He crossed his legs in the lotus position. From time to time, he sipped delicately at the drink next to him. Bogges gulped his down in two swallows. He was sorry he had, it should have been savored, it was far and away the best martini he had ever tasted.

Dr. Fall smiled. "It's a little trick I know. Would you like me to teach it to you?"

"No."

Dr. Fall shrugged. "Perhaps some other time. How did you get on with my friend Donald?"

"So you do know him."

"We talk all the time."

"What do you talk about?"

Dr. Fall sighed. "That's the journalist in you, always inquiring into other people's business."

Bogges felt abashed. He almost apologized.

"Morrow-Graves will write an extremely flattering profile. You made quite an impression. My felicitations." Dr. Fall took another sip. "And now, to work. It is remarkable, don't you think, that he who brought the light to mankind was born almost precisely to the day eleven hundred years after Theodosius banished it. What a fine, fat baby he was too, a pleasure to see. Why, you couldn't help but laugh if you saw how that delightful infant took to his suck, greedily, lustily, an insatiable thirst, he quite wore out his wet nurse, let me tell you. His parents thought the nurse was taking too much salt in her diet and that it was running through her milk. They put her on a strict regimen, but it made no difference to young François. He drank and he drank and he grew and he drank some more."

"François is a French name," said Bogges suspiciously.

"So it is and so was François, who was born in Chinon in 1490, son of Maître Rabelais."

"I think," said Bogges carefully, "that the only thing more ludicrous than calling the author of *Gargantua and Pantagruel* the savior of mankind is to claim that a Frenchman could be the Messiah."

"The French would not agree with you, Mr. Bogges."

"That proves my point."

"You may prove as many arguments to your own satisfaction as you please. I assure you, it doesn't change the facts of the matter. Have another drink, won't you?"

Bogges looked at his emptied glass and saw that it was filled. He kept his hand by his side. "You're reduced to parlor tricks in the end. I'm not surprised."

"This is not the end, Mr. Bogges. There is no end; there's no such thing, permutations, transformations, transubstantiations, that is what is. It has been remarked that the substance of Mozart can be found in a schnitzel."

"I have no idea what you're talking about."

"I'll be happy to explain. An oak growing near Mozart's grave shed its acorns. A family of pigs, rooting in the neighborhood, fed on the crop. With the acorns, the pigs swallowed some of the herbage fertilized by Mozart's decomposing body. His substance thus passed into the pigs, which became, in their time, cutlets, consumed with relish by the fine folk of Vienna. From composing to decomposing, genius persists."

"It's his music that survives, and that's what genius has to do with life."

"Your views are persistently one-sided," said Dr. Fall dismissively. "I had thought that, by now, you might have come further. However, and be that as it may, let us return to the subject at hand. You were speaking about the earthly paradise with Morrow-Graves, if I'm not mistaken."

"Not seriously."

"Ah, but I believe you were serious. Tell me, Mr. Bogges, is it not pre-cisely tricks and jests and wit that you take with the utmost seriousness?"

"Not tricks, no."

"We will not quibble. But if Mr. Chakravarti is a jest, surely you will allow the same for my little gesture with your glass."

"And the point?"

Dr. Fall gave Bogges a quizzical look. On his goaty face it looked more hungry than otherwise. "Point? There is no point. I only wish you to allow your imagination free play. Like Rabelais. Why, even on his deathbed, that ballocky fellow didn't lose his zest. 'Drop the curtain, the farce is over,' he said. 'I go to look for the Great Perhaps.'"

"And what is the Great Perhaps?" asked Bogges.

Dr. Fall wagged his head. "You do not have, at present, the faculties to comprehend."

"But you were there," said Bogges. "You were there and you fell. In other words, you were thrown out!"

For some reason, Boggs found this formulation a source of comfort. Dr. Fall narrowed his eyes. There was a red glint in their black depths.

"It became no longer appropriate for me to abide there. Not," Dr. Fall added with a twinkle, "that there is any there. In that respect, eternity re-sembles Oakland."

"Put it any way you like," said Bogges.

"It's the simple truth."

"I thought you said the truth is never simple."

"No, I said the truth is never insipid. The truth is playful. The truth of Lucifer's Fall, begging the question as your mythmakers insist on doing, the truth is I did not wish to remain; nor was I wanted."

"Why weren't you wanted?"

"Why was I no longer wanted? Because, my dear fellow, I laughed out of turn."

"Why wasn't it your turn?"

"It was never my turn first."

"What did you laugh at?"

The reply came slowly. Dr. Fall lingered over every syllable. "Everything. I laughed at simply every thing."

Bogges thought he heard laughter somewhere, a roaring in the atmosphere, like an ocean clearing its throat before launching a second flood. It was appalling. Bogges gathered himself together.

"I don't think you laughed. I think you mocked."

Dr. Fall reacted to these words with such contempt that Bogges could feel the malice.

"What you think, or think you think, is a matter of indifference. Pride goeth before the fall, quote, unquote. That old chestnut! I wasn't the spirit of pride that day. It was The Old One. He was the Prideful Spirit. The overflow of being that your little friend Marina calls love, I assure you, it had the aspect of incorporeal sewage. He was just showing off. But I wasn't laughing at His vanity. He had made a joke, the first joke, and I laughed, the first laugh. It was delightful, and too utterly funny. Imagine, no one had ever seen anything like it, corporeal being, clay. It had never occurred to us that created being was possible. Credit where credit's due, we uncreated ones never would have thought of it; The Old One had come up with something absolutely new. But the best part of the joke was still coming. The Spirit passed over that grotesque phenomenon, and the clay was quickened; it became animate; it began to breathe, in out, in out, pant, pant, gasp. It was killingly funny, a caricature of The Spirit, a send-up of Being. It would have been blasphemous if it hadn't been so hilarious. I was laughing with Him, not at Him. Of course, He didn't see it that way, The Great Humorless One. And the consequences, we could see those right away: time, ebbing and flowing, beginnings and endings, things that are and then suddenly are not. I quite liked it. It was ironic, beautifully grim. I was grateful for the diversion. He was not diverted. He expected us to take it seriously. The consequence was that po-faced cheerless naysaying virtue-oh-so-and-so's became all the fashion. Just like that Hebrew prophet. That was another one who never laughed. And he called himself the Son of Man, indeed! Rabelais, on the other hand, he was in fact as advertised, abstractor of the quintessence and full to overflowing with Pantagruelism, which, I will remind you, is a certain lightness of spirit confected of a contempt for fate."

"It's an attractive attitude," Bogges admitted.

"It is," replied Dr. Fall with satisfaction, "no less than freedom itself."

"I've noticed before you're prone to exaggerate," observed Bogges.

"And you, Mr. Bogges, are sometimes humorless. It can be deadening; it can kill. Humor is the only refuge from what you've got coming to you; it is detachment from cause and effect. Here, let me show you."

Bogges found himself suddenly under a black sky picked out in silver, stars brilliant and profuse. He thought that he had somehow stumbled out into his own backyard: the crabgrass and the trash, as well as the tumbledown fence, the shattered tools, broken helves and crippled blades, ax, spade, shovel, trowel, and the ground, hard-packed, clayey dirt, all this looked like his yard. But then he noticed a well. It had a border of rocks and a rough wooden cover. There was also a trough, and some sheds, and a coop from which birds were cooing. And there was an odor: rotting flesh, manure, urine, animals and their hides, a miasma one moved in as well as breathed in. Moreover, this yard was bigger than his. A noise and another source of stink caused Bogges to turn. A man wider than tall in a brown smock and wooden clogs emerged from a substantial stone building. In the light from a low doorway, a wavering yellow light that cast distorting shadows, the man's thick features were exaggerated, leprous. His odor suggested no bath since baptism. The man made for the coop. He reached in and captured a fat pigeon. He pinched its neck with his thumb and forefinger and then split open the bird with a knife he drew from his belt. He scooped the offal onto the ground and, leaving the mess where it fell, stumped back into the dwelling, plucking the feathers from the carcass as he went.

"Rabelais is inside," said Dr. Fall.

Bogges opened his mouth to speak. Dr. Fall waited expectantly. Bogges realized that in response to the questions he had, Dr. Fall would only take the opportunity to deliver yet another tiresome lecture; how the past is always with us or some further nonsense. Bogges shut his mouth and approached the building. He stopped before a window of thick, clouded glass framed in wood and set close to the ground. Inside, he could see a timbered room with a fine old chimney and an ample fireplace. The pigeon was already spitted and roasting over the fire. Two men in chain-mail shirts were talking quietly in a corner away from the fire. Helmets, of a dull-colored metal, very battered, were placed on a little table between them. Several other figures, clad in leather jerkins and rough homespun cloth, were seated on benches before a long board on trestles. They drank from clay cups and tore hunks of grayish bread from an enormous communal loaf. They were red of jowl and cheek, forehead low, eyes heavily lidded. Slack jaws revealed black stumps and raw gums. They were Breugel-peasant brutish. At the head of the table, in an armchair nearest the fire, sat someone of an altogether different sort. His forehead was high and creased; his eyes were large and warm. He had a beaky nose over a red, sensual mouth. He was wearing an archaic velvet cap with four rounded points drooping down like sausages in place of a brim. What Bogges could see of his hair was graying and close-cropped. A thin, equally close-trimmed beard followed the line of his jaw. A somewhat thicker moustache grew down to his chin. It was a face of great individuality. It suggested both intellect and humor. The overall effect was that the owner of the face possessed immense charm. Bogges supposed that this was François Rabelais. As he watched, Rabelais was served the pigeon and a small white loaf of his own. He attacked the pigeon and the bread, licking his fingers between mouthfuls, flinging the bones at the fire with pleasure and drinking copiously from a goblet which he constantly refilled from a flagon sheathed in straw. When the loaf and the pigeon were gone, he called for more wine in a strangely accented, musical French. This archaic sound was pleasant to Bogges. Rabelais turned with a benevolent smile and spoke to the peasants farther down the trestle.

"Good cheer, my friends, I wish you the best of good cheer. Drink, drink, as the prophet prophetically prophesied, for in this year the blind will see but little, the deaf will hear less, and the dumb will keep their wisdom to themselves. Drink, I say, for the rich will be in better circumstances than the poor and the healthy more comfortable than the sick. Drink up, then drink it down, drink heartily, for old age will be incurable on account of years past. Innkeeper, more wine for my friends!"

Wine was brought. "Your health, mon seigneur," said the peasants.

Rabelais beamed. "Health, very good, we will drink to health, for drinking is healthy and there is no wine more intoxicating than health. Indeed, it is unhealthy not to drink, for the unhealthy life is as lifeless as a life without wine, and is it not equally evident that a lifeless wine is dead? Let the dead bury the dead, and let the dogs of the Sorbonne drink lifeless wine, that is, water. But we will drink of the wine that brings warmth to the head and the heart and the John Thomas, true stiffening wine like the fine frothy stuff served up at a certain marriage at Cana in Galilee, wine that comes by its warmth honestly, warmth derived from the sun when it ripens the grape with its sweetness. Ah, to see the grape ripening in the laughing sun, it's enough to make oneself laugh out loud and that, my friends, is why we drink. For man is the laughing animal and wine, being a stimulant carrying the essence of laughter, stimulates laughter. Laughter is the Hippocratic tonic, the balm of Galen. It balances the humors and brings into harmony blood and phlegm and black bile and yellow. Laughter is health, and the laughing animal is most healthy when he laughs!"

It was impossible to determine what the peasants had made of this speech. They'd shown a respectful attention, but without the kind of interest that suggests comprehension was also involved. The two soldiers had barely looked up from their conversation. The innkeeper came back into the room and presented Rabelais with the bill.

"He's broke as usual," whispered Dr. Fall gleefully. "Watch what he does next."

Rabelais took up the bill and studied it. "A fair account," he pronounced, waving the paper and letting it fall to the floor. "A fair account for a handsome repast, and handsome is as handsome does. The accounting comes punctually, and punctuality is the courtesy of kings. And who is more courteous than our king, the good François Premier, who is as punctual at his meals as he is at collecting taxes. And what a pleasure it is to see him collect his taxes!"

The mention of taxes had captured the peasants' attention in a more focused way. The two soldiers also had looked up.

Rabelais continued: "Taxes are a beautiful thing; where would the noble and the strong, the good and the beautiful, derive their strength and beauty, their nobility and richness of soul, without the mulcting of the poor, the ugly, the weak, and the foolish? And how would you, you peasant laborers, sheepherders, draymen, cowherds, threshers, profligates of your own sweat, where would you be without the example of those who harvest that sweat, and first and foremost our good King?"

One of the peasants, possibly the youngest, although, on account of wear and poor diet there was no youth down along the trestle, spat on the floor and gibbered. Rabelais made a gesture of benediction.

"Blessed taxes, what a blessing they are to you, phlegm hawkers, spitting images of God. First, because it is more blessed to give than to receive and our King, wishing in his generosity to see that you are blessed, taxes you so that you may give and be blessed. Does not our good language by homonym and antonym and cognate etymology say that a blessing is a wound and so you are wounded in order that you may enjoy the blessing? And when your substance is transferred from your purses to the treasury of the king, you are transubstantiated and partake miraculously of the higher being of the Royal François!"

The two soldiers had been listening with greater attention. At this last remark, they stood up, fitted their helmets, marched over, and laid their hands on Rabelais.

"You are under arrest for lèse majesté. Come at once. You are to be transported to the King."

Rabelais got up without a word and, smiling to himself, was led from the room. Outside, one of the soldiers barked an order. A groom appeared with horses. The party mounted. The innkeeper came out waving his bill. Rabelais and the soldiers cantered off into the night.

"You are no doubt wondering what will happen," said Dr. Fall encouragingly.

Bogges pretended indifference. "Not particularly."

Dr. Fall chuckled. "But it's of particular interest. That rascal, that incorrigible Rabelais, or as one of his English admirers called him, the Reverend Rabbles, he is a great pal of François Premier and, as I mentioned, he's presently without funds."

"So?" said Bogges.

"So? Although he could afford neither to eat nor get to Paris, he has contrived to do both. He and the King will have a good laugh over this one!"

Before Bogges could reply, he found himself outdoors again but in bright daylight. An expanse of lawn sloped down to a wide and placid river which curved around the slope in a broad arc. There was an immense quiet which made one grow quiet inside. Bogges turned his gaze away from the river. Near the top of the slope, Rabelais sat on a stone outcropping. Bogges walked a few paces to take a closer look. His gait, he noticed, was easier, less stiff. Whatever trick Dr. Fall might be playing on him, he hoped this part of the hallucination would last. Not that this seemed like an hallucination. The sense of reality was stronger than everyday experience. The hill and the river and the man all seemed brighter, more vividly defined.

Rabelais was writing on a scroll balanced on his knees. In the lovely peace, so unmodern, Bogges could hear the scratching of the quill as it moved across the parchment-like paper. Rabelais would frequently stop to dip the quill into a curious inkwell on a rock beside him. This inkwell was in the form of a delicately carved bowl like a folded calla-lily petal gripped between the muscular thighs of a horned and goat-footed satyr. The satyr wore a lascivious smirk, as if he were reading from the scroll with enjoyment. From time to time, Rabelais took a pull from a wineskin, then loudly smacked his lips, smiled contentedly, and recommended writing.

As Bogges watched, something began to take shape, like an object emerging from a mist, like a thought forming. It was a building of five, perhaps six sides. It was impossible to tell from the spot where Bogges was standing. At each point, a circular tower rose up. Bogges counted the towers and could see that it must be a hexagon. He thought at first that it was a fortress, it was very large, but then he changed his mind. All about the slate roofs and down to the lead coping, gargoyles and animal figurines appeared giving the effect of something friendlier than a fort. A graceful arch opened in the wall facing Bogges, and he could see within an alabaster fountain. On top of the fountain the three Graces spouted water from their mouths and eyes and ears and breasts and every other orifice. Bogges and Rabelais simultaneously laughed out loud at the absurd fountain. Now the courtyard became peopled with men and women of extraordinary beauty, talking, laughing, reciting poetry, singing and playing on musical instruments, throwing balls and dice, playing at archery, strolling, sitting, standing, lying on the grass, alone, in couples and groups of three or more, holding hands and walking arm in arm, all dressed in magnificent clothing of every description, furs and silks and thread of gold and thread of silver, long robes and doublets with stocking hose, pantaloons, breeches, and short skirts like aprons, and colors rich and bright, blues, yellows, reds, crimsons, and greens. One could see by their faces and the grace of their movement that they didn't give a damn about anything petty or mean and that nothing was difficult for them. A voice, Rabelais's, said that in the Abbey of Theleme there was only one rule: Do What You Will. Bogges supposed all this was utopia, Rabelais's version in any event. It was lovely. But it seemed to Bogges that something was missing.

At this thought, he found himself back in his living room. The vision of Rabelais had been taken away so abruptly that Bogges guessed he had again disappointed Dr. Fall, who was no longer in evidence. Bogges shrugged and began climbing the stairs trying, without success, to feel light on his feet.

CHAPTER EIGHT

Bogges stood in the lobby of The Washington Oracle waiting for the elevator. He watched with vague intention the entrance of the tall redhead from Life and Styles. She covered fashions in personalities. Her trim figure, long neck, and narrow waist punctuated by roundness of calf and hip suggested a slender, perfectly proportioned hourglass or retort. She held herself effortlessly. Except for the sidelong glance, in case anyone of importance might come within range, her tread was so smooth, so gliding, that her torso showed no movement. From the waist up, she might have been a statue. In the three years that she had been employed by the paper, she had never once nodded, smiled, acknowledged Bogges's existence.

"I was like in awe of your story, Eustace. It was like awesome."

The dazzling smile that accompanied this declaration held a welcome that was hardly at all diminished by the thinness of her lips.

"And Lance's profile, it was so sensitive of you to like let him have it. I went what a great job."

Bogges smiled without answering, increasing the impression of generosity. The redhead, Bogges couldn't remember the name, Zoe, Kimberly,
Amber, Epstein, Moynihan, Myczlesweski, took the smile for approval and
encouragement.

"Yeah," she said, "great job. He's like real pro." Amberzoekim pretended
to think. "But, you know, I went, there's something missing. I mean, Lance
didn't like capture the whole Chakravarti, like the complete man, what
makes him, his tastes, his passions, his, well, like his soul."

She smiled this time with downcast eyes, as though she would be embarrassed if anyone thought she pretended to know what a soul was, or
used the term lightly, or often. It was a shy smile. Bogges permitted himself
a leer. Kim, Bogges had decided it was Kim, looked back, still smiling, but
with a different kind of shyness. There was a wistfulness in the turned-up
corners of her small green eyes and the down-turned corners of her small
crimson mouth. Perhaps there was longing as well. The elevator doors
opened. They stepped in. Although they were alone, Kim stood very close.
She wore no perfume, had no bodily scent at all.

"I want," Kim hesitated. Bogges beamed. "I want to like talk about soul
with you, Eustace. I think that you'll like understand."

Bogges laughed. Kim, no, it was Zoe, Zoe glared and then instantly al-
tered her features, resumed control. She laughed.

"I sound silly, I know. But, I think, really now, like seriously, Chakravarti deserves something more, a sympathetic ear, someone who understands
how men think. Like, isn't mind your own business really an invitation?"

Bogges admitted that from a certain point of view, it might be.

"Do you think he'd like let me interview him, like in depth?"

"He's gone out of town," said Bogges.

"When he like comes back," said Zoe caressingly.

"I don't think he's coming back."

"I could like go to him."

"I have the impression he's inaccessible, you know, some remote hill station in the Himalayas."

"I've always wanted to like see Mount Everest."

"Kashmir, yes, he's gone to Kashmir. You know there's a lot of fighting going on there. His village is right in the middle of it, he told me, terribly dangerous. I know that he'd think it would be unchivalrous to invite a lady into harm's way."

Zoe narrowed her already fairly insignificant but glowing eyes. She had decided on strong-arm tactics. "That sounds like a lot of sexist bullshit," she said.

Bogges pretended to be puzzled. "Oh, I hope not. After all, you were the one who brought up the soul."

"What are you talking about?"

"Well, Chakravarti is a very spiritual kind of guy. He's always caring for his soul by minding his own business. Being chivalrous is part of that, you know, it's chivalrous to mind your own business, and vice versa."

This made no impression. The woman spoke in a carefully neutral tone that was yet full of import. "JT thinks it's a good idea if I profile him. Mr. Thersites agrees."

Bogges now noticed that the self-deprecatory like had been dropped. The elevator opened at his floor. He stepped out. "Mr. Thersites is someone whose judgment is due all possible respect," he said.

"Then you just tell Chakravarti," she said as the doors were closing, "that Allie Epski wants to profile him!"

"Oh, that's who you are," said Bogges.

In the hall, people who didn't customarily greet Bogges smiled. Some even said good morning, spoke his name. Apparently, the man on the way down was now a man on the way up. Bogges wondered if this was how many careers advanced. His career took another step forward when he entered his office. A computer stared blankly from his desk where his Hermes 3000 had once so solidly sat.

"Would you like me to show you how to get started," asked Japrowski kindly from the corridor.

"No."

"Really, all you have to do is turn it on. It will pretty much tell you the rest."

"Where's my machine?"

"In the dumpster probably, unless one of the maintenance staff retrieved it."

"Let's go look." It took all of Bogges's self-possession to pronounce the words without a tremor. His voice was unnaturally high.

Japrowski caught the tremulous note. He laughed. "Come on, Eustace, you had to give it up sometime. By the end of the day you'll wonder how you ever got along without the computer."

Bogges understood that he was behaving childishly. On the other hand, that made no difference to what he was feeling. He gave Japrowski a look of hurt betrayal and went down to search for his typewriter. There were two dumpsters in the service alley that ran alongside the building. One gave off powerful odors of decomposition. He chose the other. This had a pleasant smell, of fragrantly moldering paper and, perhaps, inky ribbon. The dumpster's metal cover was folded back on its hinges, the edge level with the top of Bogges's head. He spotted a wooden packing crate nearby. He dragged it over, climbed up and looked in. The expanse of trash suggested nothing of interest on the surface. Bogges hung his jacket on one of the rods projecting from the end of the dumpster, rolled up his shirtsleeves, and attempted to throw a leg over the side. As he had never been able to raise his leg above his waist, even in nimblest youth, he soon gave this up. He heard a garbage truck backing down the alley. Then the grind of the reversing truck was overlaid by thunder. The sky turned dark. A breeze, cool, holding unspecified promise, blew down the narrow passage. Full-blown fall was grumbling in. It began to pour, a thick, heavy shower seasoned with urban filth. The truck backed all the way up to the first dumpster. A man in overalls jumped down from the truck and directed it backwards with important gestures. He pretended not to see Bogges. Bogges took out twenty dollars and waved it at the garbageman. This caught his attention.

"I think my typewriter is in there."

The man in overalls looked at Bogges with malice. He sniffed, directed the truck back the final few feet. Bogges took out another twenty.

"Hold up, man," called the man. The driver put the truck in neutral.

"I ain't going to go digging through all that trash for no forty bucks," he said to Bogges.

"I don't think you'll have to," Bogges replied. "It was thrown out last night or early this morning. It should be just below the surface."

"It'll cost you a hundred."

"Forty now, forty more if you find it."

The man took the bills, maintaining an expression without warmth, hoisted himself into the dumpster, and a moment later stood up with the typewriter. Bogges took out two more twenties and made the exchange. Neither of them said thank-you.

Back in his office, Bogges put the computer on the floor and restored the typewriter to its proper place. He wiped it down and called a service to come give the mechanism a chemical bath. Typewriter God propitiated, he turned his attention to the day's news. Bogges enjoyed the pleasant emptiness he experienced reading the daily offering as well as the mild satisfaction to be derived from doing his duty. All of this evaporated when he cast his eye over the lead story: *President Trump Proposes Bureau of Personal Responsibility: Mind Your Own Business Czar to have cabinet rank; 800 number for federal workers set up; private industry encouraged to institute similar measures.* Bogges didn't have the heart to read further. He filled his page and went to lunch early.

After lunch, Bogges decided to call it a day. The wait for the bus home wasn't long. As he paid his fare, the front seat across from the driver was vacated. They managed several blocks before the bus broke down. The driver was cursing the depot mechanics as Bogges descended at Farragut Square. Bicycle messengers were clustered at the feet of Farragut's statue; pigeons roosted on his head. Neither the pigeons nor the messengers appeared to notice the black poodle as big as a Great Dane planted foursquare in front of them watching with a crimson gaze Bogges descend. Bogges gave the monster a look and hurriedly turned to climb back aboard, but the bus, roaring to life, drove off without him. Bogges turned again to face the dog. There was no honor in allowing death to take him from behind. He stood waiting as solidly as he was able. At least his legs weren't visibly trembling.

But the fixed glare of the dog seemed to be staring beyond him to some distant object. Bogges made his legs move, past the messengers, past the pigeons, past the dog. Now his back was to them. He crossed the intersection of Connecticut and K. Attaining the sidewalk, he paused to look over his shoulder. The dog had vanished.

Ordinarily, the movement of traffic, the crowds going in and out of office buildings, restaurants, shops, the noises and odors, the sense of intent bustle, all these would be stimulating. But the black dog haunted him; he felt he was bearing him on his chest. Life and movement were oppressive. Nevertheless, Bogges slung his jacket over his shoulder and set off up Connecticut Avenue. He was instantly confronted by a face of pits and craters and reddened bumps with white and yellow eruptions. The poor man had his hand out. Bogges put his remaining change in it. An aged woman in stiletto heels tottered out of a jewelry store. Her legs were pencil thin and sheathed in black stockings that were yet transparent enough to reveal complicated blue veins. Bogges didn't avert his gaze in time to miss her face. Rheumy eyes outlined in gray had a shock-wide stare as though a flashbulb had just gone off. White pancake makeup was not quite heavy enough to conceal her rosacea snout. Bogges didn't need to see the scars behind her ears to know why her mouth was stretched in an immobile grin. The death's head noticed Bogges's fascination. The skin stretched imperceptibly. It appeared to be an invitation. He shuddered past. Bogges decided to keep his eyes on the ground. He tried to watch his feet and did manage to see the tips of his loafers when they cleared the end of his belly. He wished he had put on heavier shoes that morning. He continued on like this, watching the ends of his shoes flicker into sight and then disappear. The effect became hypnotic. Bogges began to drowse. It was a pleasant sensation, as though his legs were taking him for a ride. His eyes half shut. His head nodded. He lost his balance, stumbled. His eyes snapped open and his arms flew out to embrace a lamppost. He held on while his heart slowed from canter to trot. He let go before he was altogether ready only because onlookers were gathering. Home was a long way off at a Bogges pace. A drink was a good idea. Moreover, his feet hurt. There was a cobbler next door to a bar. He left his loafers off with instructions to put on the thickest soles they had and went next door. A sign warned no shoes, no shirt, no service. But it was dark inside and Bogges didn't think anyone would notice; still, he was sorry when he stepped in a puddle on the way to the bar. The bar was mostly empty. An old drunk was siting in front of whiskey and beer mumbling to himself. Farther down, a young woman sat between two young men who were standing, leaning over her and talking over her in exuberant voices. These were the only other customers. While Bogges was waiting for his drink, the old drunk, with infinite caution, began the process of getting down from his bar stool. Bogges watched with sympathy. When the old drunk had attained the floor, he stood for a moment bent over the stool, straightened with infinite care, wobbled, steadied himself. He began walking with precision, a slow-motion goose step to the bathroom. At this point, Bogges's martini was delivered. When he looked up, the old drunk had advanced as far as the youthful party at the far end of the bar. Here progress was blocked by the first of the young men. True, his back was turned to the old drunk, but then why didn't the other one facing him say to step aside? The old drunk half raised a hand in a bewildered gesture. The two young men continued to talk.

"We'll offer a chump portion and close the deal."

"Cash flow will take care of the primary note. We can service subordinated debt with working capital long enough—"

"For us to cash out. Correct."

The old drunk made another futile gesture. The two young men pretended not to notice. Bogges realized they weren't pretending. They hadn't not noticed. No, they were indifferent.

"Insider costs mean better than a ten thousand percent return on equity."

"We'd still do OK with a private placement. It'd be a hell of a lot faster."

"Less disclosure."

"Due diligence sucks."

"Yeah, piss on the SEC, we're not greedy!"

This was apparently a good joke. The girl joined in their laughter. Meanwhile, the old drunk was wobbling again, this time from his efforts to contain the urgent need. The girl glanced at him and turned her attention, veiled eyes, insistent mouth, back to the young man facing Bogges. Bogges decided he could do with a pee. He hoisted himself down and padded over.

"Excuse me," he said to the back of the young man.

This elicited no response. The girl was talking about the bad time she'd recently had with a diving instructor in Cancun.

"If you won't step aside I will walk over you," said Bogges pleasantly.

Three young faces turned with a slow, weary lassitude, expressive of the tediousness of the interruption. They gave him a look of boredom. Bogges drew back his lips, exposing canines and incisors.

"It's up to you," he said.

The young men made their blank bored faces blanker, more bored.

"It's not worth it," said the girl suddenly.

This allowed a graceful way out. Or, perhaps, they just couldn't be bothered; it really wasn't worth it. The young men turned their backs and took a step forward to the bar. Bogges allowed the old drunk to stagger past. He followed, careful to avoid lurking pools of fluids. Bogges emerged before the old drunk. The young men were again standing in the passage. As Bogges approached, they seemed to hesitate. He decided not to give them the courtesy of begging their pardon. But they took a grudging half step out of the way. When the old drunk reappeared a few minutes later, he was in better shape. In fact, a transformation had occurred beyond general tidying up. His gait was natural. His voice, when he ordered the young men to step aside, was deliberate and firm.

"Thanks for the help," he said to Bogges when he'd settled back behind his drinks.

"Glad to be of service."

"May I buy you one?"

"That's not necessary."

"What you did wasn't necessary."

"I thought it was."

The old drunk laughed. He waved in the direction of the group down the bar.

"This generation is the most self-centered, ill-mannered, bullying bunch of empty suits I've ever had the misfortune to meet. I know the old always say the world is going to hell and it's all because of the young, but these thirty-somethings really are different. They really are worse."

Bogges thought of JT. "Yes, they are different. Underneath the surface, they're still shallow. I think it has to do with not yet having encountered the melancholy discrepancy, the distance between what you think you are and what you are. It's a puerile sense of infallibility. But they aren't showing any signs of growing out of it. I expect spending their lives in front of computer screens also has something to do with it, imaginative atrophy, intellectual suffocation, indiscriminate stimuli, aspects of contemporary existence not worth examining in detail."

For some reason the old drunk became agitated. He looked at Bogges with an intense scrutiny. His forefinger tapped a tattoo against his shot glass.

"You're not a regular here, are you?"

Bogges's heart sank. He wanted to get his check. He searched in vain for the bartender. It looked like he was going to hear the story of the old drunk's disappointing life. This proved not to be the case.

"If you have the time, I'd like to tell you the story of how this bar got its name."

"Sure."

"It used to be called St. Pancras Station. The owner was a bad-tempered French woman named Danielle. We always called her Madame. By the way, my name is Penelope."

Bogges assumed this was not his first name. "How do you do, Mr. Penelope. My name is Bogges."

"Pleasure to know you, Mr. Bogges. Well, as I was saying, Madame was a piece of work, built like a sofa, never bathed, smelled of armpits. She always wore sleeveless dresses, you could see the tufts of hair peeping out under her arms. She had a sharp tongue too, abusive as hell, couldn't keep help for more than a few months. And tight, she measured out the drinks with an eye-dropper."

"She sounds like a nightmare," said Bogges. "Why did you come?"

Mr. Penelope was taken aback. "I was a regular, you understand."

Bogges supposed he did understand, up to a point; it was part habit, and the other part was the special status a regular has, or thinks he has, in a bar. Mr. Penelope had lost the thread of his narrative. He drank to collect himself.

"Cute little pest, no bigger than your foot. A miniature dachshund bitch, it was the only thing in the world Madame loved, I can tell you. Her name was Victoria. Well, Madame used to feed Victoria everyday around three o'clock, you know, when the bar had emptied out after lunch and before the happy-hour crowd came in. She'd put Victoria on a stool facing the door so the dog could bark a warning if a customer came in. Then Madame would go into the kitchen and cook up something nice, a piece of liver or a kidney or a heart, organ meats, cheap and savory.

"On the day in question, Madame placed Victoria on her stool, went back into the kitchen, and put something on the grill. While it was cooking, Madame left to attend to a call of nature. She was gone longer than expected. Meanwhile, the aroma found its way to Victoria's keen little nose. I like to think of Victoria torn between hunger and duty. I imagine her head twitching back and forth, her liquid eyes now on the street, now turned to the source of those enticing smells. Finally, animal need won out. She jumped down from the stool and sped to the kitchen. A chair stood conveniently near the counter next to the grill. She jumped, and her forepaws scrabbled on the seat bottom before sliding off. A second and then a third time she failed to gain purchase. The sound of searing was now added to the maddening smells. Victoria was frantic with hunger. She gathered her hind legs under her and made a tremendous leap. She gained the chair and then the counter. She leaned over. She licked at a succulent bubble of fat. Her tail wagged, her entire hindquarters shook with delight. It was fatal. The counter was splattered with grease. Victoria slipped snout first into the flames and was consumed.

"Madame was devastated. She sold the bar. I was the one who suggested the name to the new owner."

Bogges had the feeling Mr. Penelope had played a larger part in the story than this version suggested. However, he only asked for the name.

"I thought you knew. It's called Victoria's Grill."

Bogges allowed Mr. Penelope to buy him a drink. Then he felt obliged to return the favor. This exchange of courtesies happened more than once. During the last round, Mr. Penelope taught him the traditional bark, which all the regulars used when ordering. It was dusk when Bogges left Victoria's Grill. The cobbler shop was dark and the door was locked. He banged on it anyway but gave this up when an alarm went off. He walked in the direction of Dupont Circle, hoping to flag a cab. He'd had no luck by the time he'd reached the circle. At least his feet weren't hurting him. They felt rather numb. A panel truck with a crucifix painted in red on the side had been parked on the grass inside the circle. Soup and sandwiches were being dispensed to a dozen or so ragged men. Bogges stepped off the curb to cut through the circle. He miscalculated the depth and staggered across the street. This business of walking without shoes would take getting used to. The largest man Bogges had ever seen, or at any rate the largest man Bogges had ever seen wearing suede sandals and wooly socks, broke away from the soup kitchen.

"Say, brother," he said, "how about a hot meal and the good word?"

It was an enthusiastic, bubbling voice. It was also somewhat furry, muffled by the enormous moustache covering the giant's upper lip. The giant drew closer. He sniffed at Bogges, twitched his nose.

"Drink is the Devil's milk, brother. You've been suckling at the infernal teat."

"Mind your own business," growled Bogges, his voice hoarse from barking.

The giant planted himself squarely in Bogges's path. He might have been seven feet. He seemed to block out what little light was left in the sky. "But I am minding my business, brother. My business is to love my neighbor." He clapped a hand like a bear's paw on Bogges's shoulder. "Now, brother, we're going to get some wholesome food into you. And when you've sobered up a little, I'll take you back to the mission and get you cleaned up and find you a pair of shoes. And then, when brother ass is all looked after—that's what we call the body, brother ass—why when he's been fed and watered and shod, well then, we'll get started on your soul. It looks like to me that that soul of yours could do with a little TLC.

The bear paw on Bogges's shoulder began pulling at him.

"Get the hell off me."

"That's the Devil's talk, brother."

"Nonsense, he doesn't sound like that at all."

The authority in Bogges's voice made the giant stop short. He removed his paw. "Let us get on our knees and pray, brother."

"I'm not your brother."

"All men are brothers, and I am my brother's keeper."

The giant sank to his knees with an alarming series of popping noises. Bogges thought this was a good time to make his escape. But the paw shot out and forced him down.

"Let us pray."

The man's strength was irresistible. Bogges resisted anyway. Some of the ragged men, having finished eating, wandered over.

"He's got the spirit on him now," said one.

"Lord, lord, save this poor sinner," bubbled the giant.

Bogges writhed and twisted under the iron weight of the man's hand. His eye fell on Daniel Chester French's fountain in the middle of the circle and fastened on the beautifully rounded breast of the maiden in three-quarter relief sculpted by the master.

"Breast," breathed Bogges. It seemed comforting under the circumstances.

The hand twitched on his shoulder.

"Breasts," repeated Bogges with more force. And then, for good measure, "Breasts and cunts."

"Right on, man," shouted one of the onlookers.

"Breasts and cunts and asses and legs," chanted Bogges.

The iron hand shook.

"Long, long naked legs."

The giant moaned softly.

"Long, naked legs unchastely spread, then wrapped and gripping."

"Go, man, go," said the onlookers in chorus. "Get down, get down."

"Perspiring torsos, twisting and writhing," chanted Bogges.

As if to illustrate, Bogges twisted and writhed himself. The hand fell away. The giant seemed to be weeping. He had covered his face.

"Lordy lord," spoke the chorus.

'Lord, lord," beseeched the giant antiphonally.

Bogges got up carefully. "Long, blissful caresses," he said. "Thrusting pleasures." He took a step. Then another. "Lips on lips, kisses sweetly wet."

The giant was still moaning as Bogges walked away.

"Probing tongues, exploring fingers," he called back over his shoulder.

"Amen, brother, amen," returned the chorus.

CHAPTER NINE

When he'd gotten home, Bogges bandaged his feet and fell asleep fully dressed on top of the undressed bed. He awoke the next morning long enough to call Morrow-Graves to say he was sick and, feeling better for it, went back to sleep. Physical ease prompted spiritual activity. He dreamt of a grassy park, of flowerbeds and little stands of trees, of a maypole on a hill and people dancing round it. They were dancing in two concentric circles, clockwise and counterclockwise. Each held a long, colored ribbon of satin, blue, red, yellow, silver, or forest green. As they danced, they wrapped the maypole until it took on a new shape, narrow at the top and spreading bell-like at the base. The maypole became a bell. The bell began to ring. The ringing became louder, more insistent. Bogges woke up and answered the phone.

"Are you feeling terrible?" asked Marina's voice.

"So, so. Who told you?"

"The most peculiar man. I called your office and whoever answered ..."

"Lance Morrow-Graves?"

"Yes, I think that's what he said. But his accent was, was, I don't know what it was, and his voice was fruity."

"That's Morrow-Graves."

"Who is he?"

"The assistant managing editor, my boss."

"Then why did he say he was in loco parentis?"

Bogges laughed. "It's the sort of thing he would say."

"Well, he did. You don't sound sick."

"I'm not."

"Then why did you tell him you're sick?"

"I had to tell him something."

"So what's wrong with you."

"I'm spending the day in bed."

"Alone?"

Marina's voice was suddenly full of suspicion. Bogges also became suspicious.

"Why? Haven't you ever spent a day in bed alone?" he said.

"If you're going to be rude, I won't invite you to our picnic."

It seemed to Bogges it had been Marina making rude insinuations. But he only said, "What's this about a picnic?" He looked at the bedside clock. "It's almost eleven-thirty. Shouldn't you be starting lunch?"

"The strangest thing happened. I got to the restaurant and checked the reservation line. We had a full book, but every single party had cancelled. I don't know what's stranger, that everyone cancelled or that everyone took the trouble to call."

Bogges thought he understood. A terrifying notion came to him. What if minding your own business meant that you had to cook for yourself. Had he eaten his last lunch? Could he support Marina's operation on his patronage alone? His mind full of thoughts of lunch, he asked again, "What's this about a picnic?"

"I'm going to pick Hugo up from nursery school and take him to Montrose Park. Can you meet us?"

"How will I get there?"

"Well, even though it's uphill, it's only five blocks from your house. I suppose you could walk."

"I can't walk. That's why I'm in bed."

"Why can't you walk?"

Explaining to Marina that he'd walked home without shoes from Dupont Circle and was crippled weighed like lead on his spirit. "Never mind. I'll see you there."

"We'll try to get a picnic table near the boxwood maze; you know where that is?"

"Yes."

He swung his legs around and his feet touched the carpet. They seemed to be alright. He stood up. So far so good: they were able to bear his weight although, he reminded himself, the carpet was thick. He began to think about which pair of shoes might accommodate feet, bandages, and socks. He moved over to the bedroom closet, dancing gingerly, without frolicking, and inspected the rack of shoes. The brown wingtips might work, but tying them would be a problem. He decided to deal with that later, after the problem of bathing. He went to run the bath and while it was filling realized with incredible foresight that he would have to change the bandages. He checked the medicine cabinet to establish that he had indeed used up all the bandages last night. Bogges ran through several variations on bathing and bandages before concluding that he would settle for a shave and washing his armpits in the sink.

Feet, bandages, and socks would not all fit into his shoes. By eliminating socks he could just slide in without completely dislodging the bandages. He decided to live with the parts that had balled up under an instep. He didn't try to tie his shoes. He was in a wistful mood when he locked the front door behind himself, the prospect of lunch made him nostalgic, and why did it always seem to take so long to get out of the house? It also took a fair amount of time to walk the five blocks up to the park. The customary toe-and-heel was rendered intolerable by the state of toes and heels. Flat-footed was painful because of the balled-up bandages. He walked the rest of the way rolling from side to side. He pretended he was a sailor at sea. He was sweating by the time he reached the park. He'd have to sit downwind of Marina. He went along a brick path with picnic tables on one side and the boxwood maze on the other. The tables were bunched together, youngish mothers eating cake and ice cream with children and balloons. The boxwoods gave off a warm, close scent, tranquil, Victorian, smelling like a high-ceilinged room with odd corners, dusty wooden floors, and the afternoon sun shining through long-sealed windows, except that it was outdoors. Bogges heard a squeal from within the boxwoods.

"That sounds like Hugo," called Bogges.

"No, it doesn't," said Hugo's voice.

"Then who is it?"

"Guess!"

Bogges pondered. "It's the sound of Hugo hiding."

Hugo had been caught by surprise. There was a pause. "Woof," barked Hugo.

Bogges thought he'd try to be more playful after food and rest. "Where's your mother?"

"Woof!"

He walked through a little playground to the other side of the maze. A father was pushing a very small boy in a swing. The father was singing. "He flies through the air with the greatest of ease, that daring young man on the flying trapeze."

Marina came into view. She was sitting on a blanket spread on the grass arranging plates and silverware and napkins and glasses from a hamper. A second, larger hamper with its lid closed looked like it was waiting to be unpacked. Bogges waved and then remembered about being upwind. He stopped in his tracks, licked his forefinger, and held it up. Marina looked surprised by this greeting. Bogges realized how foolish he appeared and set off abruptly. His right foot set off first. As his left foot had come to rest on the right foot's shoelaces, he went sprawling.

Marina was there instantly. She bent over him. "Can you get up?"

Bogges smiled up into her face. "No." Then he pulled her down.

"Let go of me, you rat, what if Hugo sees us?"

"There is no Hugo, there's only Toby the Oatmeal Dog."

"He's been playing that since he made up the story Sunday night. How did you know?"

"He barked at me, and I just now remembered."

She hadn't said anything about his odor. Bogges thought this might have something to do with her being a cook, being used to garlic and onions and so on, perhaps meat that was a little off.

Marina struggled free. "We can't make love in broad daylight in a park full of people with Toby the Oatmeal Dog lurking in the bushes, so why don't you help me with lunch?" she said.

Bogges got up for lunch. "I'll unpack the hamper," he said.

"Only if you promise not to look like you're undressing a woman while you're doing it." She rose and looked down at Bogges's feet. "You're not wearing any socks."

"Well, for a picnic, you know, it's the pastoral effect."

"Brown wingtips are not pastoral, Eustace."

This did not deter Bogges one bit from unpacking the hamper with relish. He brought out smoked trout and cold partridge followed by a warm beef stew that smelled of rosemary and tomato. He had begun unwrapping the first of five cheeses when he saw Marina fill an enameled metal bowl with some of the stew.

"That bowl makes your stew look like dog food. Oh no, you're kidding."

Marina shrugged. "I'll make him use a spoon if you insist."

"No, no, far be it from me to interfere with a man's enjoyment of his meal. Or a boy's, or a dog's."

"I'll go get the little mutt," she said.

While Marina was gone, Bogges cut up the bread, a white torpedo loaf with a brown crust, no herbs or olives or nuts or sun-dried nonsense in the dough, just unassertive bread that went with food instead of dominating it, a food delivery vehicle. It was also good by itself, Bogges confirmed, although it would be even better with butter, ah, yes, here was butter cooling against the two bottles of Tavel. One bottle was for Bogges, the other for Marina and Hugo, no, there was chocolate milk for Hugo, imagine, chocolate milk and stew, maybe that wouldn't be too bad, in a Mexican way. In any event, Bogges would also drink Hugo's portion of the second bottle of wine.

"Woof."

Marina and Hugo sat down.

"Hello, Toby," said Bogges. "I'd wag my tail but, as you see, I'm sitting on it."

Hugo laughed. He held out a paw which Bogges sniffed. Then Bogges held out his paw and Hugo returned the courtesy.

"Aesthetic unities must be preserved," said Bogges to no one in particular.

There was no further conversation for the next fifteen minutes. Bogges watched with interest to see how Hugo would manage. It looked pretty much the way one would expect, a good deal of sauce on lips, nose, and chin, with a smear here and there on forehead and eyebrows. It wasn't all that different from the effect Hugo had achieved when he'd eaten macaroni with his fingers. But Bogges was impressed by the seriousness with which the child had entered into the role. When it came time to lick the bowl clean, the little tongue flickering in and out and the lapping sounds were convincing. Bogges briefly had the illusion he was looking at a boy-headed puppy.

"I need a bowl for my milk," Hugo told his mother.

"I'm sorry, darling, I forgot to bring one. I have a straw for you."

"Can I just use the same bowl? See, it's all clean."

"I don't think you'll get much that way. Why don't you pour the milk in the bowl and then use the straw."

This was a satisfactory compromise. When Hugo had finished, Marina wiped his face and sent him off to play until dessert. Bogges helped himself to the rest of the stew. He eyed the remaining bread and decided it had best be saved for cheese and salad.

"What a nice child you have, Marina. He's interesting, and he has manners."

"You mean, for a dog."

"Yes, also for a human. He's civilized, even if he does eat from a dog-food bowl. I suppose most parents would refuse to let their children eat that way. On the other hand, I bet those same parents wouldn't have taught them to give in gracefully when you meet them halfway."

"Thank you. I think children want direction; they're grateful for it. I don't know why American parents are so afraid to correct them while there's still time."

"A grammatical offense, parenting. They've turned what should be a nominative state of being into an act, and so they just act the part. Unlike Hugo, they don't know their own business."

Marina looked troubled. Bogges was sorry he'd formulated his thought this way.

"Who is this Chakravarti person really?" she asked. "I don't know why, but all this talk of mind your own business frightens me. But at the same time, I don't believe it."

She looked into Bogges's eyes. "I can believe that you're being visited by the Devil, Eustace, a lot more easily than I can believe people will mind their own business."

Bogges wondered why Marina didn't laugh. He realized that he didn't find it funny either. He also realized that he couldn't tell Marina that he was responsible for mind your own business. He hadn't known how important she was to him, important enough that he couldn't tell her the whole truth. But if she's so important to me, he asked himself, why should I hide anything from her? The question answered itself.

"It's just a silly fad," he said. "You know how people are."

"They can get dangerous when they get silly."

There was nothing to say to this, so Bogges poured some of Hugo's share of the wine into his glass. "Which cheese can I give you?" he asked.

"Some of the goat, some of the sheep, and a little blue."

A woman of good appetite and pronounced tastes, thought Bogges. "I love you," he said.

"You'd better," said Marina.

Bogges sampled all five cheeses. Then, with the salad, he finished them.

"Heigh-ho," he said. What's dessert?"

"Go get Hugo and you'll see."

"Couldn't I just call him?"

"You can try."

After awhile, Bogges got up to fetch Hugo. The father and son had vanished from the swings and the little playground was empty. He walked around the boxwoods and came to an entrance to the maze through a trellised gazebo. The birthday party had moved into the maze; there were excited voices and the sudden puppet appearance among the boxwoods of children's heads seemingly unattached to their torsos bobbing up and down. Three of the mothers sat in the shade of the gazebo. Bogges called again for Hugo. The women stared at Bogges and went back to their conversation. There was an unoccupied bench resembling a window seat built against one of the trellises. Bogges decided it would be pleasant to sit. He installed himself. Lunch, wine, warmth, the buzz of insects and young mothers' conversation, the comfort of not sitting on the ground, the boxwood opiate scent all conspired to lull him. A nap was near. But the bandages pressed against his instep. He pushed off his shoes. The bandages were hopelessly balled up. He pushed those off too and stretched his toes. If there were scabs, they didn't bleed. It was all very delightful. He would go barefoot, carry his shoes, it would save wear on the shoe leather, it was in the pastoral mode, antibiotics were for infections. He began to listen half-aware to the women's talk.

"I wish that Kimberly's school was more academic."

"She's in kindergarten?"

"No, in first."

"Already?"

"She skipped a grade. She's very gifted."

"Donald could have been in first too this year, but we decided to hold him back. Boys mature later than girls, so we thought it was better for him."

"Ben is traveling all the time."

Bogges wondered how a child could do that. He realized they were now talking about husbands.

"I hate it when Sam's away."

"Well, I miss Ben, but I like my space."

"Oh, so do I. When I'm at the gym, it's my time."

"Is Oscar still your trainer?"

"Mmm."

The women giggled.

Bogges stood up. "Hugo." Then, "Toby the Oatmeal Dog."

The women stopped talking.

"Woof," barked Bogges. "Woof."

The women became alarmed at the barefoot barking man. They got hurriedly to their feet.

"Kimberly," called one. "Kimberly Atwood-Branch." Then louder, "It's time to say goodbye."

The other mothers began calling for Donald, Sue, Jacob, Jorge, Alex, Jonathan, Nate, Raphael, Alicia, Percival. Bogges woofed. The women fled into the maze.

Hugo emerged on all fours from under a bush. "We were playing hide-and-go-seek. No one found me."

Bogges stooped with unaccustomed agility and picked him up. He took his shoes with his free hand and left the bandages as a memento. "Time for dessert," said Bogges.

"Let's eat it!" said Hugo gleefully.

Sometime later, Bogges was eyeing the remnants of the almond paste and pear tart. Hugo was asleep in his mother's lap. His mouth was open and imperceptibly drooling. While not charming, it also didn't look the same way on a four-year-old that it would on somebody older. Bogges discovered he was too full to reach for the rest of the tart. He would have liked to have put his head in Marina's lap if there'd been room. He yawned.

"Delicious, Marina, I didn't know you were a baker."

"I'm not. I bought it at the patisserie."

"Marvelous," said Bogges. He put his head down on the blanket and closed his eyes. Marina sighed. Bogges drifted off. Marina sighed more audibly. Bogges realized this was not a signal of sleep. He opened his eyes. "What's on your mind."

"Nothing."

Bogges came to the further realization that not only was something on Marina's mind but that he must draw her out, encourage her to speak. He reminded himself, now fully awake, that this did not mean that he was required to interpret whatever was said; or maybe he was. He'd have to wait and judge, see what she wanted. The main thing, he said to himself firmly, was to listen. After all, listening was an old reporter's trick. He sat back up as the first step to doing this.

"It was nice of the older children to play with Hugo," said Bogges by way of priming the pump.

"They probably weren't. Hugo just didn't notice."

"That's why they didn't find him, because they weren't looking for him?"

"Probably."

"Well, Hugo is an example to us all," said Bogges.

"You admire that kind of innocence, don't you?"

"Yes."

Marina sighed again. "Do you think that's why Dr. Fall, the Devil, is trying to possess you?"

"I don't know that he's trying to possess me."

"That's what he does, Eustace. He takes possession of your soul, and then he consumes it, feeds off it, eats it like a meal. Have you seen Father Roche?"

"No, he was going out of town."

"He's back."

"I'll call him."

"Promise?"

"I promise."

Marina sighed in a different way; some obstruction had been removed. "When I married Hugo's father I thought it was forever. Isn't that what marriage is for?"

Bogges wanted to say that was only one of the many ways marriage was supposed to be and wasn't. He stopped himself. This was wise. Marina was only drawing breath.

"You see, I thought that when two people married they didn't swallow each other. I thought they nourished each other, fed each other, loved each other. Oh, how terrible each other is when you keep repeating it, like a munching sound. How do you get away from that?"

"One another," suggested Bogges.

Marina brightened. "Yes, one another. That sounds right, doesn't it?"

"Yes."

"Respectful and affectionate, loving."

"Yes."

Marina sighed happily. "Can I give you the rest of the tart?"

"Alright."

She watched him eat. "May I ask you something?" she said.

"Of course."

"You haven't been lonely, since you and Sally separated, have you?"

"I've been alone, if that's what you mean."

"No, yes, I did mean that, but I also meant that you haven't felt lonely."

It was on the tip of Bogges's tongue to say that he didn't know, that loneliness just wasn't something he thought about. This seemed ungallant. "I hadn't known until this moment that I was lonely."

Marina looked pleased; then she looked skeptical. Then she laughed. "You are a cunning rascal, Eustace Bogges."

CHAPTER TEN

The paper was one of the first corporations to follow the president's directive.

"Lunch," said the note on Bogges's desk, "is a useful forum to develop sources. We encourage it. However, and keeping in mind expense-account imperatives, the demands of the news business require that your time be also accounted for. If you know of a colleague in need of guidance, please address your counsel to persrespons.oracle.com or call your personal responsibility advocate."

Bogges resisted his first impulse to call the number and leave an obscene message. Instead, he went downstairs to talk to Japrowski. The newsroom was full and busy but curiously subdued. Reporters and editors were intent before their computer screens, typing away as though on deadline although that was hours away. The unusual quiet made an impression on Bogges without, however, leading to a conclusion. Japrowski was also pecking away at his keyboard.

"Abel, I've got to talk to you," said Bogges.

"I'll be with you in a minute," said Japrowski without looking away from his screen. He seemed to be gritting his teeth when he spoke. Bogges looked over Japrowski's shoulder and read.

"The reason young Kingsley is not assigned to stories he deems 'important' is because he remains ignorant of the fundamental principles of market behavior, the rudiments of fiscal policy, and vast swathes of economic history. The reason he is so 'heavily edited' is because he doesn't yet know how to write. On the other hand, I'm glad that the personal responsibility advocate has brought his dissatisfaction with my performance as the editor of *Business and Finance* to my attention. A man of Kingsley's abilities and talents can only be inspired to achieve greater successes when he is put on one month's probation."

"There," said Japrowski to himself, "that will fix the little bastard." He looked up from his screen. "Now, Eustace, what the hell do you want?"

Bogges was taken aback. He had never seen Japrowski so angry; in fact, come to think of it, he had never seen his friend angry at all. "What's gotten into you, Abel?"

"Not a fucking thing. I'm minding my own business, which I can do a damn sight more effectively than Kingsley. He missed first deadline yesterday because he was so busy writing his manifesto to my incompetence he didn't have enough time to finish his piece. Not that that distinguishes him from the rest of the pissant reporters who call themselves writers here. The city desk had half its quota of copy because everyone was too busy complaining about discrimination to file. Life and Styles was two hours late shutting down because Allie Epski was getting her passport instead of finishing her overview of suburban rap roadie fashions, and the Foreign Desk ended up recycling last Sunday's think pieces as news analysis because the bureaus in Paris, London, and New Delhi declined their assignments on the grounds that they were phony questions instigated by the State Department. Of course, that was true, but so what?"

"Are you feeling alright, Abel?"

"I've never felt better in my life, goddammit. Speaking of which, when are you going to stop sleepwalking through yours?"

The only possible answer to this question was to become angry, which Bogges did in the most instantaneous and exhilarating way.

"You'll be pleased to note this sleepwalker can prepare his page, on deadline, without the assistance of pissant reporters or fucking TV screens. So since you're so fucking wide awake, I guess I don't need to tell you to fuck off."

Japrowski swivelled around and jumped up from his chair. He thrust his skinny form against Bogges's bulk. Bogges puffed out his chest, and his belly pushed Japrowski back into his seat. Bogges sniffed at him and lumbered off.

The newsroom was growing louder. Confrontations, not all verbal, were in progress up and down the aisles of desks. Three reporters had surrounded the assistant managing editor for Hispanic and Latin American affairs. They were speaking Spanish to him at a great rate, the words spraying like weapons fire, waving forefingers and poking him about the chest and shoulders, fists clutching sheets of paper bearing exclamation points at the beginning and end of every sentence. A little farther on, a female reporter took a swing at her editor. He, a diminutive Ivy League sprout half her weight and possessing about the same proportion of experience, reeled into Bogges. Bogges caught him, set him upright, launched him back.

"Rewrite that lead," he said encouragingly.

Two men in identical double-breasted suits whom Bogges vaguely recognized as editorial writers had taken off their glasses. They were nose to nose, red-faced, straining against each other. As he passed by, Bogges heard one snarl, "The page is pablum. You're supposed to have an opinion, for Christ's sakes."

"On the one hand, on the other hand, on the one hand, on the other hand," chanted the second suit. "You indecisive, verbose son of a bitch."

Obits seemed to have Morrow-Graves by the throat. Sally was screaming at JT. He bore the mark of her hand on his cheek. Bogges paused to savor this vignette. Sally turned in mid-invective. Her next remarks were aimed at her former husband.

"Why the hell did you see fit to go and print that letter?"

The hell was pronounced "hail."

"Which letter?" Bogges innocently returned.

He knew very well which letter. It had run the day before. The correspondent had congratulated The Oracle on Sally's column. He had called her discussion of human relationships in the jargon of Madison Avenue a delightful piece of sarcasm. He had further pointed out that since our most intimate feelings could be spoken of like commodities for sale, it should be a small step to the sale of actual humans in the marketplace. Perhaps we are already engaging in this exciting new twenty-first century form of slavery. No doubt this was Sally's point. So wrote the correspondent, tongue-in-cheek. Bogges had published the letter not only for its acuity but because Sally could be expected not to get it.

"How dare he call me sarcastic!" she said.

"He was being ironic," replied Bogges.

"What the hail's the difference!"

"Sarcasm," replied Bogges, "is saying the opposite of what you mean in order to belittle. It's a kind of sneer. Irony is a form of intelligence. It exposes contradiction in a paradoxical manner. In this case, by arguing from a fatuous assumption to an absurd conclusion."

"How dare he be ironic!"

"The letters page is the readers' forum," replied Bogges complacently.

"Oh shut up."

Sally led with her right. Bogges ducked. JT received the blow on the other cheek.

"Goddammit, mind your own business, Eustace!" cried JT. His handsome face looked ever more boyish from the renewed glow of his cheeks.

It was on the tip of Bogges's tongue to affirm he was minding his own business. Then something more important occurred to him. He hurried off without a word. After Bogges had closed his office door, he said in a quiet voice, "I know you're there, you bastard, come out and show your nasty bearded weasel face."

Bogges stood waiting for Dr. Fall to appear. In the stillness, he could hear the seconds tick by in his head. He tried to make the sound a presence.

When this failed, he looked impatiently at his bare wrist, pretending to consult the watch he hadn't worn in forty years. Nor did this evoke Dr. Fall. Bogges wondered if an invocation was required, some kind of ceremony involving magic circles or pentagrams and clenched fists or extended palms and foul smoke and nasal chanting and saying things backwards and prancing naked under the moon and an iron cauldron with vermin stewing in a sulfurous broth and burning pyres as well as other things along those lines. He'd be damned if he'd perform such nonsense. Maybe he should make an appointment. Then he remembered Marina's priest. Father Roche was back from wherever he'd been. Bogges called. Father Roche could see him right away. He went outside and stationed himself on the corner of the street where traffic was more or less headed in the direction he wanted. This was both a strategic and a tactical decision. Once he'd gotten into the cab, the driver would be forced to go several blocks on Bogges's way before anything imaginative could begin to happen. The cab that stopped at his signaling appeared to be from the Maiwei Taxi Association. It was hard to make out the name, which had been hand-painted on the door panels and then struck several times with a ballpeen hammer. He had just time to prevent an unnecessary turn east on Massachusetts Avenue but failed to stop the driver from continuing north on 16th Street. Bogges made a rapid recalculation of his route and instructed the driver to turn left on R Street. A dark and hawklike visage turned with an agreeable smile, revealing a prominently missing front tooth.

"Uhhrr," warbled the visage.

"Yes," said Bogges approvingly, "left on R."

"Uhhrr."

The left taken on P Street was an acceptable alternative. The tricky part would be going around Dupont Circle in the correct inner lane so as to come out heading northwest on Massachusetts. Bogges husbanded his forces. Where P emptied into the Circle, Bogges started banging furiously with his left fist behind the driver's ear.

"Left lane, left, left, left, we want Mass. Ave. No, the left lane, dammit."

A thought occurred to Bogges as they circumnavigated Dupont Circle. "We are wanting to go up Mass. Ave., which is requiring to take inner part of circle," said the voice of Mr. Chakravarti.

"Aaahhh," said the driver.

"You will now be pleased to be taking right-hand turn at next light so as to be pointing in correct direction."

"Aaahhh."

Bogges had time as they traveled up Massachusetts Avenue to ponder why the faux Indian diction penetrated. Familiar rhythms and intonations, possibly. He got out in front of a three-story house. It was of rough yellow stucco with many windows and shutters painted a dull green on a point of land where three streets met at odd angles. It was a large house, neither cheerful nor imposing. While the streets around it were thick with trees, the house stood without shade on a triangular plot. The house was bare, stark. The effect was institutional and ascetic. Bogges pushed the button for the doorbell and heard it ring. He waited a not very long time and then hammered with the knocker, which, he now noticed, was a crouching gargoyle. Then the door was opened by a tiny and ancient woman. Bogges's first thoughts were that she was the model for the gargoyle and that the streak of white over her broad upper lip was dust. Then he thought it was stubble. She wore a house-dress of some rough cloth and was fragrantly unwashed.

"I have an appointment with Father Roche."

The old crone, it was the only possible word, stood aside. Bogges entered through a wooden vestibule that smelled of moldering boots and slickers and hats and umbrellas. On his left was a dining room. A long table took up most of the area, and there were high-backed wooden chairs pushed against the wall. The chairs looked uncomfortable. The meals served would be austere.

Refectory, said Bogges to himself.

On his right was a parlor or day room, although, except for the occasional gleam at the edges, no daylight penetrated the drawn shades. It was furnished with heavy, dark pieces which were old without being antiques.

Bogges entered and turned inquiringly to the crone, who had disappeared. He turned back to inspect the room and noted a number of porcelain cats in various poses on the mantelpiece and side table. Father Roche then came in. He had a crew cut of iron-gray hair. His face was square and pale, with very clear, almost translucent skin. A pinpoint of red on each cheek gave an impression that the skin was stretched tight across the bones. He wore shiny black trousers and a black knit sport shirt with a white border around collar and cuffs, a sort of clerical leisure suit. He didn't offer his hand, but put his palms together and laced his fingers while slightly inclining his upper body.

"Mr. Bogges?" The voice was soft, dry, remote. Bogges wondered if he kept it under wraps for use on Sundays.

"Thank you for seeing me."

"You are a friend of Marina Niemalle?"

"Yes."

Father Roche motioned Bogges to be seated. Bogges chose a love seat upholstered in a greasy material that turned out also to have broken springs. Father Roche drew up an armchair very close, so that their knees were almost touching. He looked inquiringly at Bogges, who, for some reason, suddenly found himself at a loss. There was an uncomfortable silence; at least it was uncomfortable for Bogges. After a few moments, Father Roche spoke.

"I believe you said that you are being visited by the Devil?"

"Yes."

"What makes you think that?"

"Well, the visits."

There was another silence. Again, Bogges had the impression he'd had the first time over the phone that Father Roche was neither waiting patiently nor impatiently, that he wasn't waiting at all. It was like being faced by a vacuum. Bogges offered something into the vacuum.

"He calls himself Dr. Fall. He seems to know things that no one could know."

"What sort of things?"

"Well, he knew who Eve really was."

"Ah?"

"She was an anthropoid ape who lived millions of years ago. She was the first creature to achieve self-consciousness."

"What makes you think that was Eve?"

"Because he said so." This was lame. "I mean, because of the way he told the story." This wasn't much better.

"Under what circumstances were you told this story?"

"I was asleep. I was taking a nap after lunch," Bogges admitted.

Father Roche had had his elbows resting on the arms of his chair. Now he put his hands on his knees and leaned forward. "It sounds like you were having a nightmare."

"I thought so at first. Then he began appearing to me when I was awake."

"And what did he tell you then?"

"It's hard to describe, exactly, or summarize, I guess I should say. It seems to do with the history of man's being and why, or how, Lucifer fell."

"Those are large subjects."

Bogges nodded agreement. "Yes, but in a funny way, even though everything he tells me is vivid and convincing, it all ends up being small. Not trite, but facile and cavalier."

"That can be expected from the Father of Lies."

"He also told me that François Rabelais was the true savior of mankind. He even showed me Rabelais imagining what I suppose was the earthly paradise."

"And what was that like?" asked the priest.

"Pleasant, but static. I wasn't tempted, if that's what you mean."

Father Roche chose not to pursue this line of inquiry. Bogges could hardly blame him.

"Has anyone else seen your visitor?" asked the priest.

"No." Then Bogges remembered that Morrow-Graves had spoken to Dr. Fall on his doorstep. "Yes," he said excitedly, "the assistant managing editor of The Washington Oracle spoke to him."

Bogges liked giving Morrow-Graves his title. It seemed to add verisimilitude.

"Can this person confirm that he saw the Devil?"

"No," said Bogges. "All he knows is that he spoke to someone."

Bogges was again faced with the waiting which wasn't waiting. He felt disconcerted, a little ashamed. He made himself feel annoyed in self-defense.

"What do I need to say to convince you that I'm telling the truth?"

"I believe you are telling the truth."

"But you don't believe I'm being visited by the Devil."

"I did not say that. Perhaps you are having nightmares and hallucinations, perhaps not."

"What kind of proof do you require?"

"Evidence of preternatural phenomena and independent witnesses."

Bogges remembered his encounter with the two muggers. "I saw a monstrous black poodle sever a mugger's head. I think it was sent by Satan."

This sounded worse than what had come before. Father Roche, however, was forensically dispassionate.

"You witnessed this?"

"Yes."

"Anyone else?"

"Yes. The other mugger. He ran away."

"Ah."

Bogges decided to try another tack. "Dr. Fall once told me that the will is a sanctuary, that the Devil can only affect the senses. The spiritual faculties, so to speak, are inviolate."

"That is sound doctrine," replied Father Roche. "The will is man's to exercise or not, as he chooses. And of course God's."

"What do you mean?"

"I mean that God can act directly on the will."

"There's a word for that, isn't there?"

"I suppose you'd call it grace."

The word made Bogges think of Marina. He wondered if she had experienced something you might call God's grace. He rather thought she had. They didn't seem to be getting anywhere.

"Do you mind if I ask you a personal question?" said Bogges.

Father Roche nodded for him to go on.

"Have you ever seen something you thought was the Devil?"

"I have seen many things I believe came from the Devil."

"What sort of things?"

"Oh, they're all the same sort of things, at bottom, turning away from God."

"Yes, but what specifically made you think the Devil was active, operating, I mean, causing something to happen?"

Father Roche thought for a moment. "Sometimes, among a group of people, a party or gathering of one kind or another, someone will begin to gossip or tell a lie. Then a second person will join in with another lie or piece of gossip. A third will try to top that, and soon everyone is gossiping, maligning their neighbor or posturing before their friends, aggrandizing themselves at the expense of others. It's a breath of evil blowing across the room; everyone has suddenly become possessed. The tone, the spiritual tone, of the gathering changes. Where before there was goodwill and fellowship, now there's malice. Although the sense of fellowship remains, even intensifies. It's part of what makes malice so seductive, that sense that it's us against them and that we are superior. It's the fellowship of the Devil. In those situations, under those circumstances, he's there, malice spiritualized and incarnate."

"It's happening right now," said Bogges.

"No doubt."

"No, I mean the Mind Your Own Business Czar in the White House and the Bureau of Personal Responsibility. It's all my fault."

"How is that your fault?"

"You've read about it?"

"Yes."

"Well, I started it. I edit the Letters to the Editor page of The Oracle. A few weeks ago I ran a letter that said people should mind their own business."

"It's a very good idea."

"Yes. But I wrote that letter."

"I've sometimes wondered if the newspaper didn't supply its own correspondence. The letters all sound the same, like the news stories."

"No, that's my editing."

"I'm afraid I don't follow."

Bogges felt they were straying from the subject. "Look, I sometimes contribute a letter under a pseudonym."

"Why do you do that?"

"I don't know. To get things off my chest, out of boredom, as a jest."

"So you wrote a letter suggesting that people should mind their own business and the White House acted on this suggestion in a way you didn't expect and you believe that this was the fault of the Devil?"

Father Roche had a way of summing things up that made Bogges feel like a fool. It occurred to him that that might indeed be the case. "No, it's my fault," said Bogges. "But the way things have gotten twisted, that's Dr. Fall's, I mean the Devil's doing."

Father Roche sat back in his chair and put his palms together in front of his chest. He looked up at the ceiling and pursed his mouth. He looked down from the ceiling. "In what way have things gotten twisted?"

"Well, I told you that I meant mind your own business as a joke. I didn't mean it seriously."

"Perhaps real jokes are indeed serious," said the priest.

"Evidently."

"So what did you mean, in all seriousness?"

Bogges tried to think through what he had meant.

"I suppose I meant that people should tend to their own affairs and not interfere with how other people manage theirs, that people should be serious about what they do, that they should be competent, but that they shouldn't be so earnest or so self-righteous. We seem to have the worst of two worlds; few people are terribly good at what they do, and even fewer are happy doing it, but at the same time, they insist on being honored for it. Isn't that what all this nonsense about being a professional is, you know, an information-technology professional instead of a computer repairman,

a financial-services professional instead of a bank teller, a learning special-
ist instead of a tutor, customer care instead of complaints. Why, even in my
own work we're not minding our own business. We talk about the 'profes-
sion of journalism,' as though we possessed some body of knowledge that
can be expounded or applied. Perhaps a sense of history allows us to put
events in some kind of perspective. But mostly we're just reporters, chron-
iclers, making a note of what happened that day. There's only one thing a
reporter knows, or should know: how to use words honestly. But to a large
degree, we've inflated language and devalued meaning just like everybody
else."

Father Roche looked impassively at Bogges. "I take it then," he said,
"that what you really mean by mind your own business is that people
should be honest with themselves and with each other."

"Of course people should be those things. But that's not exactly what
I'm getting at, or that's not the whole of it."

"Ah, the whole of it. What, in your opinion, is the whole of it?"

Bogges sighed. "I don't know. But I certainly didn't mean that everyone
should be even more busybody than they already are."

"Are they?"

"Yes. The president wants everyone to spy on each other and complain
about each other. Isn't that what the Bureau of Personal Responsibility is?"

"Yes."

"At the office today," said Bogges, "everybody was at each other's throats."

"Your colleagues usually get along with each other?"

Bogges laughed. "No. They just usually manage to contain their feelings
better."

"Pardon me, Mr. Bogges, but I thought I heard you say that you wanted
people to be honest."

"But this is the opposite of what I wanted. This is how Dr. Fall has twisted everything. If people were really minding their own business, they'd be
too busy monitoring themselves to care much about what everyone else
was doing."

"Possibly," said Father Roche. "More than likely you're right. But what
do you propose to do about it?"

"That's why I came to you. To ask your advice."

"My advice is to confess that you wrote the letter that started all this trouble."

Bogges thought he'd already confessed. But he only said, "What good will that do?"

"I don't know what good will come of it, but I know it will be good for your soul."

Bogges was faced with the vacuum again. This time, however, he felt neither annoyed nor disconcerted. He didn't quite know what he felt. Charitably, Father Roche filled in the blankness.

"We can't know what the truth might bring. On the other hand, we see what comes from your, well, let us call it your joke."

"That's one way out, I guess," said Bogges.

"I'm not sure it's a way out," said Father Roche. "It might be a way in."

"You sound like Dr. Fall."

"I'm sorry if I do. What reminds you of him?"

"I don't know. I suppose the suggestion that bigger things are at stake, just beneath the surface."

"Don't you think that is indeed the case?"

"Not always. Sometimes things are just what they seem to be."

"But you did not ask to consult me because things are just what they seem to be."

"No."

"So why are you here, Mr. Bogges?"

This sounded so much like Dr. Fall that Bogges almost bolted. "I'm here because," said Bogges with a great effort, "you're a priest and I'm being visited by the Devil and priests believe in the Devil, and because the Devil has told me that death comes to all men and that the only way to make myself free is to become well, playful."

"But, Mr. Bogges, all of this is true," said the priest with a smile. "Although I would prefer to say that we must make ourselves God's plaything."

"So you agree with Dr. Fall."

"Certainly not."

"It sounds like you do."

"Then I apologize. We work with the same material, but we draw different conclusions. You see, that's one of the restrictions the Devil works under: he can only deal with what is. It emphasizes his nothingness."

Here, Father Roche quietly began to laugh at what was, evidently, a theological joke.

"I told him once he was a nothingness," said Bogges.

"You were quite right to say that. How did he reply?"

Bogges thought back. "He said that he didn't care what I called him so long as I was conscious of him."

"Yes, he hates not being acknowledged."

"He said that his greatest triumph was making people disbelieve in his existence."

Father Roche shook his head. "He lies."

"Perhaps I should refuse to acknowledge him, entertain his presence?"

"That is always a good idea. However, once you let him in, it's difficult to send him away."

"He said something along those lines to me also."

"Yes, he would say that."

"So I could send him away if I wanted to?"

"Perhaps. Tell me, Mr. Bogges, do you want to send your visitor away?"

"I don't know."

"Ah."

"I suppose you couldn't exorcize him, could you?"

"No. Under the circumstances, no. Have you considered seeing a psychiatrist?"

"That's what Dr. Fall claims to be," replied Bogges.

Father Roche got up and walked over to a fairly adequate imitation of a Spanish writing desk and took a phone book from a drawer. He looked through the pages and then put it back. "There is no Dr. Fall listed in the white or yellow pages," he said.

"I know. Would it have made any difference if he was?"

"I think so, yes. A liar or a pathologically disturbed person might have fastened on an actual psychiatrist, perhaps his own psychiatrist, as a satanic figure."

"At least you don't think I'm disturbed."

"Mr. Bogges, only a fool is not disturbed."

"Pathologically, I mean."

Father Roche shrugged. "I'm not a psychiatrist. On the other hand, I suspect a psychiatrist might very well diagnose someone who believed he was being visited by the Devil as deluded and in need of treatment. Perhaps you should consider seeing a psychiatrist who's listed in the phone book."

"I think I'm getting all the psychiatric attention I want."

"I understand your dilemma."

Father Roche offered his hand. It was impossible to determine if this was a gesture of friendship or simply of dismissal. Bogges got up with his customary difficulty and took the hand.

"Why don't you let me know," said the priest, "how things develop."

CHAPTER ELEVEN

"Nah, can't go that way."

Bogges kept his temper. The driver's reply had been a rational response to his directions back to the office, at least so far as hearing the words he had spoken and replying to them in a way that suggested their meaning had been grasped. "But that's the most direct way," said Bogges.

"Don't make no difference. Downtown all blocked off. Get you near as I can."

"Why is the downtown all blocked off?"

"Dee-moan-strayshions."

"What demonstrations?"

"Don't rightly know. Radio say, folks be protesting, nobody be minding their own business."

Bogges was about to inquire further. Reporters always talk to taxi drivers. It's how, in a strange town, they take the pulse of the electorate, determine what the common man is thinking, hear what was on the radio without having to listen to it. Bogges remembered that he was not in a strange town nor still a reporter. He held his peace until the taxi was waved over by police at Sheridan Circle. An officer spoke through the driver's window.

"I'm afraid you'll have to continue your journey on foot, sir. You," he said, addressing the driver, "will circle around and proceed north on Massachusetts."

"How far down is it stopped up, officer?" asked Bogges.

"All the way to the Capitol."

"Shoot, can't go nowhere. Ain't no business to be done. I'm goin' home," said the driver.

"You will circle around," repeated the officer, "and proceed north—"

"I know, I know. I think I can find my own way home after driving this here cab for fifty-five years without you directing me twice."

Bogges paid the driver. Because he seemed to know his business, Bogges gave him the full fare and a good tip too. When he'd gotten out, he saw that the police had managed to keep the circle clear. Farther on, down Massachusetts Avenue to Dupont Circle, a tide of humanity surged and eddied as aimlessly, or as purposively, as waves breaking on the shore, or stands of trees bending before a wind, or perhaps herds of bison grazing on the plain, or vast flocks of sheep ruminating in a meadow. No, thought Bogges, it was more like rush-hour, workers going to work or colonies of seals rousing themselves when the seal-hunters brandish their clubs or, perhaps, lemmings heading for a cliff. It was like rush-hour because of the way everyone looked; their expressions were grim and, in a weak way, determined. Except, it wasn't like rush-hour because no one was going anywhere or perhaps that was like rush hour, in a sense.

Bogges plunged in, breasting the crowd and sometimes elbowing it. He put on a Russian scowl, dark, woeful, heavy with memory and portent. This was sufficient to cow the Rumanians, who had exited their embassy and were milling about while trying to keep from getting jostled and still look as though they were part of whatever was going on. Other embassy folk, truculent Turks and, from across the street, glaring Greeks, edged closer to one another. Bogges pressed on. Four old codgers buttoned into

three-piece suits stood behind the iron gates of the Cosmos Club, survey-
ing the crowds. They drank from highballs and, when they thought no
one was looking, took ice cubes from their glasses and pitched them at
the mob. Two men clad in leather pants and leather vests open to shirt-
less chests were communicating in sign language, their hands fluttering
like butterflies. A ragged posse of bicycle messengers had encircled a sleek
young fellow speaking German into a cell phone; the consonants sounded
like gravel crunching underfoot. The messengers had pointed the antennas
of their walkie-talkies in his direction and were fiddling with the controls.
When the right frequency was struck, a screech was emitted from the cell
phone. But the sleek fellow only talked more earnestly into the phone.

Farther on, the Hilton had emptied itself of its guests. The cleaning staff,
led by a fireplug of a woman in a maid's uniform, were making threatening
gestures with brooms and mops and toilet plungers at a tour of aged men
and women. These, identically shod in white athletic shoes, were unbuck-
ling plastic belts as quickly as their arthritic fingers would allow, perhaps to
defend themselves, perhaps to surrender.

Bogges was drawing closer to Dupont Circle. The crowd grew more
dense. He encountered a group of heavily made-up girls in short skirts of
nylon or cellulose. They had burning cigarettes in their hands. When they
noticed Bogges, they exhaled contemptuously in his direction. He managed to push through onto the circle. The mass of bodies was crushing. He
looked up, craning to see above the crowd. The giant of the soup kitch-
en had scaled the fountain. His enormous arms stretched almost half way
around the massive central column. He was clinging to the sculpture of the
maiden. His face was pressed close. He seemed to be nuzzling her breast.
Dangling from his arms and legs, a number of the homeless were tearing
and pulling at him. The giant kicked out. But no sooner did he shed one of
the men than two more sprang up to worry him. One of these shinnied up
his trunk and began beating him about the head chanting "Mind your own
business, mind your own business."

Someone else, a coffee boy from the Starbucks across the street or,
possibly, the clerk from Kramer Books who had once prevented Bogges

from copying down the complete recipe for hot dogs and sauerkraut from a cookbook he wasn't going to purchase, one of these, or someone else, took up the cry. The crowd, which had been largely silent, now began to chant, but not in unison, more like a round. Own Your Mind, Business Your Business, Business Own Mind.

A corporate lawyer or lobbyist swung a heavy briefcase in rhythm to his own version and struck Bogges full in the belly. Bogges doubled over and then was shoved from behind. He fell face forward, and just then the mob began to move. Feet trod on his calves, thighs, a shin was scraped, a hip bruised, a rib lacerated. Bogges struggled to stand. A kick at his back knocked out his wind. This prevented Bogges from rising. More shoes and heels and an occasional heavy boot battered at him. He put his hands over his head, but not in time to fend off a blow to the ear. He felt blood on his neck. The mob was too thick on the ground to move very fast, but Bogges thought the pace was quickening. There were more kicks, and greater momentum behind them. The other ear began to bleed. Breathing became difficult. Then the blows stopped. A space had opened around him. Dr. Fall asked if he needed a hand up. Bogges got up on his own by hands and knees. His rear end was too tempting a target for someone. Bogges was back down on the ground in an instant, but retribution was equally swift. An animal howl, high pitched, keening, was followed by the sight of a severed ankle and foot, like a shoe tree in its tasseled loafer. It sailed over Bogges's head. Bogges got up quickly and looked at Dr. Fall's victim. He looked away after seeing a writhing form and a lot of blood but not before taking in the expression on the man's face.

Dr. Fall laughed.

"All illusory, as the Buddha teaches. You will note that our friend here remains bipedal. Not that that will make him feel any better. Thus, the power of illusion."

Dr. Fall smiled again, benignly, although his beard somehow gave the smile a self-satisfied, smarmy cast. Bogges looked again at the figure on the ground. Indeed, two oxblood-colored shoes with, presumably, feet in them, emerged from two blue pants legs. The man seemed to be in his thirties and ordinarily in blooming health. A thick mop of shining chestnut hair suggested this. The way it fell over a high white forehead suggested the man took pride in his looks and took great care of them. Of course, it was hard to tell what he looked like at present. His screams distorted his face and were almost too horrible to be pitiable.

"Yes," continued Dr. Fall, "there's no convincing him that he hasn't lost that foot. What he needs now is a good psychiatrist."

"For God's sake," said Bogges, "do something for the poor bastard."

"As you wish," said Dr. Fall.

The next moment, the screams stopped. The man jumped up. He stared at Dr. Fall. A look of cinematic terror passed over his face. He really was strikingly handsome. Then he disappeared whimpering into the crowd. Dr. Fall took Bogges companionably by the arm and they too began to move. The space which had protected them now preceded them, or the crowd parted before them. The arm Dr. Fall was holding was numbed with cold. Bogges pulled free. All around them, office workers in suits and store clerks in smocks, society ladies and derelicts, marched and counter-marched, their mouths working, their expressions set. But no sound carried. Bogges had the impression he was in a diving bell. Not only sound was muted. Vision was lightly blurred, as if he and Dr. Fall were swimming through an aqueous solution.

"I've got to get back to the office," said Bogges.

"But my dear fellow, why?"

"Why? Because I've got a deadline to meet."

"Today, all deadlines were suspended. Today, there is no news."

"That's ridiculous. Look at all these protesters. It's a hell of a big story."

"When a tree falls in the forest and there's no one to hear it, does a tree fall in the forest?" asked Dr. Fall conversationally.

"What are you talking about?"

"There's no story when there's no one to interview and no one to report it, wouldn't you agree?"

"Why is there no one to report it?"

"Your colleagues have all gone home."

"Well, I'm here!"

Dr. Fall shrugged. "Try interviewing someone yourself."

The space shrunk to the little patch of ground Bogges was standing on, and he found himself pressed on every side and surrounded by noise. He stopped a middle-aged man in a sports jacket with leather patches on the elbows.

"I'm Eustace Bogges of *The Washington Oracle*. Would you tell me what you're protesting?"

"Mind your own business."

Bogges next stopped a woman in a chartreuse jogging suit who didn't appear to consume the minimum daily requirement of calories.

"I'm Eustace Bogges of *The Oracle*."

"Mind your own business."

He tried several others, many of whom shoved past without bothering to recite the slogan. The crowd was beginning to thin. Bogges confronted a little man with a Van Dyke. He started to identify himself.

"I know who you are, Mr. Bogges," said Dr. Fall. "They're all going home. Why don't we get a drink?"

He led Bogges to a bar. It was in a shallow cellar set a few steps below the pavement. They entered, and Bogges climbed onto a stool covered in red vinyl studded with brass nails. Barstools seemed to be the one kind of seat he could get on and off without too much effort. Dr. Fall walked around behind the bar, reached for bottles and ice and shaker, and began mixing. The bare brick walls exuded a moist stink, beer and cigarettes, perhaps vomit.

"Open the door if it bothers you," said Dr. Fall.

Bogges thought he could put up with it. "Where's the bartender?" he asked.

"With everyone else, of course."

They were alone in a subterranean dimness. The television was broadcasting news. As Bogges watched, President Trump appeared. He was sitting behind the desk in the Oval Office.

"My grandfather, great gentleman from Germany, great innkeeper, beautiful staff, all beautiful beautiful women, the best, he said work will set you free. So, everyone go back to work." He spoke in his characteristic petulant snarl. "Mind your own business means making money. The Saudis have taken over the top floor of the Trump Grand, and they expect room service. Jared and Ivanka can't do this by themselves."

Then the screen went blank. Dr. Fall brought drinks.

"What's gotten into everyone?" Bogges asked.

"The Devil knows," sighed Dr. Fall.

"That's just what I thought."

Dr. Fall began mixing a second round. "Perhaps a little more vermouth this time?"

"I suppose you're going to send me another bill?"

"Naturally."

"Because the patient doesn't sufficiently value the services if he's not charged."

"Therapy, not services."

"Whatever," said Bogges, cursing himself for using the idiot juvenile tag.

Dr. Fall grinned a fiendish grin.

"Don't be sarcastic," said Bogges.

"What, about my charges, never, I assure you. I take them with the utmost seriousness. How else would I live?"

"You don't have a choice?" asked Bogges with interest.

"It's a life," replied Dr. Fall.

Bogges drank from his newly made drink. "And, considering the alternative, it's not all bad."

"Exactly."

"Since I'm paying for this, I want some answers."

"Please. Today, the drinks are on the house."

Bogges looked annoyed.

Dr. Fall relented. "You're taking this all far too seriously. I couldn't help pulling your leg."

"Thanks for not tearing it off."

Dr. Fall disregarded the crack.

It occurred to Bogges that Dr. Fall did not appreciate sarcasm when it was directed at him. "Everyone looks like zombies. What's gotten into them?"

"Nothing has gotten into everyone, and so, for once, they're able to agree on something, left wing and right wing, Democrats and Republicans, radicals and centrists, Southerners and Northerners. Why are there no counter-demonstrators? Because they have all finally found the one thing they can agree on, the one thing that brings them all together: nothing. They're free, thanks to your, or Mr. Chakravarti's suggestion, free to celebrate an orgy of nothingness. Of course, no one knows what to do with freedom except rebel against the daily grind."

"Except for Trump. He's still at work."

"I'm sorry, ethics will not allow me to discuss another patient."

"This nothingness as you call it," said Bogges after a pause, "is really an emptiness. Socrates, the great ironist, examined himself according to the Oracle's admonition and found that he knew nothing. From that he began the search for first principles and became the wisest man in Athens."

"Yes, Mr. Bogges, and his greatest gest was allowing the Athenians to execute him. His rich friend Crito had arranged to get him out of prison and out of Attica. Socrates refused. He chose death. This decision was his most profound irony because by allowing the people he had annoyed or made fools of to kill him, he proved that it is precisely the people with no sense of irony who live the most ironic lives."

"So all those people protesting and demonstrating and chanting mind your own business, they're not going to work anymore. Is that what you mean?"

"Of course not. They'll all go home and turn on the TV and, when they find there's nothing on, they'll become bored. Tomorrow," continued Dr. Fall, "they'll all go back to work for lack of anything better to do."

"What nonsense. There are plenty of better things to do. People will go back to work because they have to earn a living."

"I suppose so." Dr. Fall seemed to yawn. "But tell me, Mr. Bogges, do they have to do it to get ahead? Do you admire them, these career climbers? Do you know that the only thing that spiritualizes them is gossip."

Before Bogges could respond, Dr. Fall pronounced in organ tones, "Emphatically not. As the heir to Rabelais, how could you?" He looked slyly at Bogges. "You are his heir, you know. In the truest, the most essential way, you are his heir." When Bogges didn't immediately respond he added, "That is why you are of such great interest."

Like most, Bogges did feel that he was of great interest. However, he wasn't willing to admit this, certainly not to the Devil. "Give me another drink," said Bogges.

"I'll join you."

Dr. Fall busied himself behind the bar again, and Bogges wondered how the little man could be at eye level. He peered over the bar. Dr. Fall was standing on a wooden, trellis-like platform. He also seemed to be wearing elevator shoes. Vain little phony, thought Bogges. Dr. Fall glared at him but said nothing, not that he needed to. Bogges felt he could hear Dr. Fall's thoughts as clearly as Dr. Fall could hear his.

"So what am I thinking about?" asked Dr. Fall pettishly.

"Nothing."

"Wrong!" shouted Dr. Fall gleefully. "Wrong, wrong, wrong!" He stamped his foot with such force that Bogges thought he might tear himself in half, like Rumpelstiltskin. "Not a chance," said Dr. Fall. "That was a fairy tale."

"What about the fairy tales you've been telling me?" asked Bogges.

"Projection is one of the more straightforward delusions of neurosis," replied Dr. Fall irrelevantly.

"Don't try to sound like Father Roche."

"It's inevitable. We work with the same material."

"But you draw different conclusions."

"In principle, yes. For example, it was his god who insisted that you render unto Caesar the things that are Caesar's."

"And who is your god?"

"Freedom."

"Freedom from what?"

"Freedom to, my friend, freedom to."

"I am not your friend."

"Whatever."

"Freedom to do what?"

"To do whatever. You'll have to admit, doing what you will is no longer fashionable. It was your ancestor Rabelais' dictum, do what you will, but who reads him now? Who follows his teachings?"

"Rabelais is not my ancestor," said Bogges. "I have no French blood, thank God."

"Blood," replied Dr. Fall, "who said anything about blood? I speak of soul and soullessness, rich souls and bland souls, well-seasoned, tasty souls, souls of a complex and subtle fragrance and souls of blancmange, of white bread, souls with no savor of their own, production-line souls, modern souls."

Dr. Fall stared at Bogges with a peculiar expression. He looks hungry, said Bogges to himself. Dr. Fall instantly assumed a milder aspect.

"How did we get from Rabelais," asked Dr. Fall rhetorically, "from learning and energy and appetite and playfulness, from the highest expression of man to the wage and profits slave, the emptiness of man today? In brief, from the skills that were acquired casting the great bells of Notre Dame and Chartres and all the other Gothic cathedrals there developed certain metallurgical techniques that were first applied to the casting of cannon and, ultimately, to the manufacture of the engines that powered the industrial revolution. It was no accident that the sound that once called men to prayer led to the sound of men laboring in the satanic mills. Although, there really is nothing satanic about a factory. On the contrary, what would the angel of play have to do with wage labor? Blake didn't know what he was talking about."

"I don't know what you're talking about," said Bogges.

"You are being disingenuous. You know instinctively what I'm saying. You know because you have appetite and because your soul has savor."

Again, the hungry look, but this time Dr. Fall recovered without pause.

"Credit where credit's due. In fact, it is all about credit. The Renaissance was the fork in the road. Rabelais was the right way. But man took the wrong turn. He trusted in credit instead of play; the gold and silver from the New World financed the wars that spurred the innovations in armaments that developed the techniques that built the factories that leached the play from men's souls. And as the world grew richer and less playful, the ancient learning that was all about the nature of the soul was found to be not relevant. The real purpose of learning was taken away so that all might learn, technical learning, professional learning, learning so that all could get a job, so that money could be earned. That is why the good citizens of the District of Columbia are wandering around like zombies muttering 'Mind your own business.'"

"That's it?" said Bogges incredulously. "That's the history of man from the Renaissance to now?"

"In a word, or a few dozen words, yes. The tragedy of man is the history of capital, except it's not a tragedy: it's a farce. Look what's happened today. Everyone has stopped, momentarily, thinking about money. But money is what gives form to the bland nothingness of their souls. And so, without form to their nothingness, they become null and void. Today politics came to a dead halt because pollsters can't measure public opinion; everyone is keeping their opinions to themselves. Lawyers have shut up shop because no one can be bothered to sue their neighbor for the simple reason that neighbors can't be bothered to disagree. The police won't catch any criminals today because thieves and robbers have stopped thinking about money and can't be bothered to steal. Teachers have stopped teaching and students have stopped learning; what would be the point if you no longer want a job? The ad agencies have closed for the day. The lobbyists and the legislators, the salesmen and the licensing clerks, they've all gone home."

"This is just the world of commerce," Bogges said. "Poets and artists and scholars and musicians, people who do things because they're valuable in themselves and not for the sake of something else, these people haven't quit and gone home."

"What makes you think that? Do you believe anyone does what they do honestly anymore? Look at yourself. Didn't you have to become Mr. Chakravarti to speak what was on your mind? In other words, didn't you have to become dishonest in order to commit truth? At least you did it in a spirit of play."

Bogges decided it was time to start drinking. He drained his glass, and it was full again.

"I offer you the unending cup," pronounced Dr. Fall. "I want you to tell the history and meaning of man. You will write so that your readers, and all will read you, will feel what Eve felt when she first knew herself, what Sadyattes thought when he woke from his dream of the shower of gold and what he foresaw when he invented coin; your readers will be lulled by Jesus's poetic delusion and glory in the fierce delights of Theodosius's power. They'll sigh for the sweetness of Rabelais's vision and cringe at the Industrial Revolution. You will tell my story."

"You want me to be your ghost writer," said Bogges.

"No, no, you will write under your own name; they will be your words, and you will write without effort. The words will come like a purling stream, and they will be always the right words, the veritable logos. And you will never go out of print."

"I hate paperbacks," said Bogges irrelevantly.

"You will not go into paper in your lifetime."

"How long is that?"

"Many, many editions."

"And afterwards?"

"The long sleep."

"What about dreams? Will there be dreams?"

Dr. Fall looked away. "Have another drink," he said.

"No. Answer me. Will there be dreams?"

"Possibly. It all depends."

"Depends on what?" Bogges spoke fiercely.

"I'm not allowed to say."

"Why?"

"There are certain rules I also follow."

"Since when?"

"Before the beginning, Mr. Bogges."

"What rules are these?"

"The rules of what is and what is not."

"Why is it that every time I ask you a real question, you answer with an emptiness?"

"What do you expect? Your questions are fundamentally meaningless. I try to do the best I can with the material you give me to work with. Perhaps this will satisfy your curiosity. There are as many possibilities in death as there are in life, and, like life, they are all essentially the same. Now please, I insist that you have another drink. See, your glass is full."

"It was already full."

"Whatever. Listen to me, Mr. Bogges, and the world will listen to you. Your slightest pronouncement will be heard, pondered, honored. You will be everywhere there is man. You will be known as the Author."

"I prefer anonymity."

"Very well. You will be ubiquitous, but without an address. You will be a god."

At these words, Bogges felt an electric shock, an enlargement of self, a mighty growing into his true girth. He seemed to himself to tower over the past and the present of mankind, and from his great height he surveyed a future in which, well, in which Jonah Thomas would be respectful and Sally Benton would keep her distance and Lance Morrow-Graves wouldn't maunder in his presence. Of course, this would be multiplied ten thousandfold, all the Jonah Thomases of the world would be respectful, all the Sally Bentons awed, all the Morrow-Graveses silenced. He supposed there would be wealth too. Perhaps he would buy a car, although that would entail learning how to drive. And all that was required of him was to take dictation from the Devil.

"Not dictation," said Dr Fall. "The muse will speak through you."

To Bogges's disgust, Dr. Fall's clipped gray hair turned honey-blond and curled radiantly down his head. The hooked nose straightened and grew delicate, the thin, hard mouth, already red, became soft and voluptuous. The black glaring eyes turned a limpid blue, shaped like almonds. The transformation to an exquisite maiden was almost complete, except that the Van Dyke remained like graffito on the now softly rounded chin. Then it began to vanish from the face.

Bogges spoke when only a shadow lingered. "Your tricks are repugnant."

Dr. Fall resumed his customary aspect. "No tricks, Mr. Bogges. I am whatever you want me to be."

The voice was wistful. It struck Bogges that Dr. Fall was lonely. This set off an entirely new train of thought. "What happened to you that day you laughed?"

"Since it was apparent that I was the only one who could properly appreciate creation, I came here."

"Were you the only one?" asked Bogges. "To come here, I mean."

"Well, let us say that I'm the only one who takes a consistent interest."

"I've often suspected that was the case."

Dr. Fall laughed. "Believe me, Mr. Bogges, you're much better off with me taking a hand in things. Those others, sycophants, always climbing the golden stair, they're not much fun."

"You have your sycophants too," replied Bogges.

"Yes, and I admit that a little fawning every now and then can be pleasant but, just between us, my crew can be equally tiresome. In the end, these careerists are all pretty second rate, not for the likes of you and me."

Bogges began to congratulate himself on this shared disdain. Then he recollected who was doing the flattering.

"So what?" said Dr. Fall.

So what, indeed? After all, thought Bogges, these are my views, this is how I feel and think; so what if my views are shared by the Devil? Does that make these views infernal? Although, Bogges admitted to himself, one could hardly call scorn and disdain graceful. Graceful, however, was a word one could not associate with Eustace Bogges. It wasn't in his nature to be graceful. On the other hand, he could appreciate it when he saw it. In Marina, for example. Some of her views were absurd, of course. Bogges didn't doubt for a moment that Dr. Fall, despite his reputation for lies, had given an accurate account of things, according to his own lights. That was the problem though. One more or less agrees on the facts, but one can draw any number of conclusions from those facts. Take the story of Eve. Bogges was perfectly willing to agree that human consciousness arose from an episode of suicidal narcissism. It made sense. He could see evidence of it every day and all around. Nevertheless, it was equally evident that other things could be done with the story. What had Father Roche suggested? God was the better bet. But why bet at all when the Devil offers a sure thing? Father Roche or Dr. Fall, one or the other, but why does it have to be one or the other? Bogges was reminded of that annoying poster he'd seen, it seemed a lifetime ago: if you're not part of the solution, you're part of the problem. It was the same kind of argument, at bottom. What a lot of nonsense. He was getting tired of it all, especially of people who argue that way. The fact was, God and the Devil appeared to need him a lot more than he needed them. Well, they could fight it out nicely without Eustace Bogges. Or maybe they couldn't unless he was in the middle. Possibly that was one of the rules Dr. Fall and Father Roche were so fond of alluding to: you're automatically part of the fight. We'll see about that, said Bogges to himself. He would avoid foreign entanglements, as George Washington had advised. He'd simply take himself out of the picture. He'd refuse to entertain their presence. He'd withdraw. That would fix them. God and the Devil would have to work it out on their own; they'd have to make up. He washed his hands of the matter. He thought of what that sly fox Rabelais had said on his deathbed: I go to look for the Great Perhaps. On the whole, Bogges was with Rabelais. Devil take it, he'd mind his own business in his own way. He wondered if he'd be allowed to get away with it.

Bogges got up from his bar stool. He did it without thinking, willing himself. He heard Dr. Fall's breathing behind him. Why does he bother? thought Bogges.

"Aesthetic unities. I'm a great believer in the requirements of art."

Bogges's hand was on the doorknob.

"The offer stands," said Dr. Fall.

Then Bogges was outside. The street was empty. Grayish clouds scudded before a dull glow in the west. The streetlamps came on. He hurried past a branch of his former bank. The door was open. It was evidently deserted. It occurred to Bogges that this would be a good time to make a withdrawal. He turned back and entered the lobby. His footsteps were muffled by carpet, his breathing magnified by the domed ceiling. He opened a little

waist-high wooden gate that allowed access to the tellers's cages. He walked
along behind the glass until he found a drawer that hadn't been shut. He
took nine hundred-dollar bills from the drawer and scribbled a note on a
teller's pad. *IOU nine hundred dollars. Signed, Grippin Fall.* Then he shut
the drawer and heard it lock. He was sorry he hadn't remembered to put
the note in the drawer. He laid it on top. He wished he could remember Dr.
Fall's account number at, what was the name of the bank in Switzerland?
Schweizer-Deutsche Bank für something or other. He wrote that down too.
He pocketed his cash and went across the street to Kramer Books.

The cookbook he wanted was out of reach, probably to prevent brows-
ing. He went to grab a chair from the little café in back of the store and saw
the better part of a quiche on a platter on the service counter. It would go
bad by morning if someone didn't do something about it. He retrieved the
cookbook and the quiche, and ate while he read. Caraway seeds appeared
to be the missing ingredient in the sauerkraut recipe. His interest was
caught by the one following, an elaborate version involving juniper ber-
ries and white wine and goose fat and pork chops and ham and frankfurt-
ers and boiled potatoes. It had a French name but was nonetheless worth
copying. Perhaps he could get Marina to make it for him. Then it was time
to finish the rest of the evening's business. He put the cookbook back on a
shelf at eye level and went out into the night.

The streets were silent but for the sound of an occasional rat scrabbling
in the garbage and the scrape of his own tread. He walked past bars and
restaurants and shops and the glass and steel office buildings that were
built over them. Their doors had been left open, and no one had bothered
anywhere to turn off the lights. A wisp of stale air would breathe out at
him from the lobbies. His way was illuminated by a stark, science-fiction
glare, as though he were the lone explorer on an empty planet. Bogges
found he was telling himself a story: When Gesgob landed in the capitol
city of Planet X, his mission was to discover what had happened to the
featherless bipeds who had inhabited its once-thriving civilization. Everywhere Gesgob looked there were signs of great undertakings, exhortations
to action of a nature yet to be determined, carcasses of varied gradations

of sentience evidently readied for some kind of ritual sacrifice in specially designed spaces, and much foodstuffs heaped and hung in numerous halls devoted to this purpose. Gesgob entered one such hall and fed. He noticed strange markings on a portion of his meal and, perhaps it was a clue, copied the markings for further investigation.

madeinthailandfor

poloralphlauren

Bogges burped. The quiche, he decided, had gone unrefrigerated too long. He pushed aside a shopping cart a derelict had left in front of the paper's entrance and climbed the steps to the lobby. He walked along the corridor past the empty offices of his colleagues. Hours ago, someone had left a pot of coffee warming on an electric element. The coffee had been reduced to an essence. It's sour odor could be felt on the tongue. It tasted of the required task, to be accomplished late at night, alone, under a harsh light. He unlocked his office door, entered, and sat down before his typewriter. The familiar act of rolling in a sheet of paper helped him to compose his thoughts. He pecked out his byline with a forefinger and then went through the ritual of writing the lead: think what the story is about, reduce that to a sentence, and you're off.

Washington shut down yesterday and history stopped while citizens from every walk of life took to the streets in an inchoate protest against pretty much everything.

Bogges x-ed out *inchoate* and substituted *spontaneous*, decided on *spontaneous* and *inchoate*, then went on to report the day's news. An hour later, he wrote, now with both forefingers, the closing paragraph.

S. J. Chakravarti, who said he is retiring to an undisclosed location for his own safety, admitted some responsibility for what might be seen as an episode of mass psychosis. "On the other hand," he said, "no one who was truly minding their own business would behave this way. Clearly, the Devil has taken a hand in the matter."

Bogges was sorry he'd had to bring Chakravarti into the report, but he must get rid of him somehow. He hoped this final dishonesty wouldn't compromise the effect of his deliberate gesture. He pulled the last sheet of copy out of the typewriter and re-read the story from the beginning. When he was done, he went down to the museum in the basement.

The museum, maintained for tours of the paper, was in a modest room holding the few remnants of pre-offset press, pre-computer days. A lino-type machine, a chase in which to set the type, and a hand-operated proof press were on display, demonstrating to schoolchildren curious primitive technologies. The actual presses, which had massively occupied a sub-base-ment running below an entire city block, had been dismantled and sold for scrap. Bogges's plan was to print several hundred copies of his story in the form of fliers on the proof press, break into vending machines and fill them, drop off bundles at drug stores, perhaps also the White House gates. He'd use the derelict shopping cart he'd found coming in for his deliveries. That was the plan. It wasn't much of a substitute for a real paper. On the other hand, the other hand was nothing.

In the elevator, Bogges tried to remember the sequence for printing: he must first get the melting pot hot for the lead ingot; once the ingot was molten, tap out the story on the linotype keyboard; when the ma-chine spewed out the slugs and lined them up in their tray, set the type in the form known as a chase; reconcile the lines; slide the chase onto the cart called the turtle and wheel it over to the proof press ... Oh God, he'd forgotten that the linotype keyboard wasn't arranged like the typewriter's qwertyuiop, it was, it was, it was etaoin shrdlu; and wasn't that vertically? He'd be at it all night, amidst the fragrance of hot lead, silvery shards from the slugs scattered around his feet, picking out the words on that impossi-ble, that perverse keyboard. These thoughts had brought him to the door of the museum. Dr. Fall, in a printer's leather smock which looked to be from the era of Franklin, possibly Gutenberg, greeted him.

"I think we can do a hell of a lot better than that, Mr. Bogges."

"What are you doing here?" asked Bogges.

"Where else would I be at this time of night? After all, the daily news-paper is one of my finest inventions."

"You invented newspapers? I'm too tired and too busy for your incred-ible nonsense."

"It is altogether credible. It wasn't so long ago that western man began his day reading the Bible. I thought it would be more appropriate to substitute the ephemeral for the eternal. Luckily for you, most people seem to agree." Dr. Fall brushed his fingers against his smock, examined his nails. "We have a deadline to meet, and as I don't mind taking dictation, we will go upstairs and I'll transfer your story to the computer so that we can get out tomorrow's paper."

"How are we going to do that?" said Bogges despite himself.

"If you understood anything about computers, you'd know that with a few keystrokes I can send your prose to the plant in Maryland and that the pressmen, who are standing by, will then start the presses and put out the paper. After that, the carriers, who are now gathering at the plant, will deliver the entire paper to all 527,342 daily subscribers!"

"I thought every one had gone home to mind their own business."

"Not the printers and the carriers. They come as soon as I call. I'm organizing a union, you know."

Bogges had been vaguely aware that an attempt at organizing a union was afoot. He remembered now having overheard some management type blaming it on the Devil. He was suddenly more sympathetic to whatever Dr. Fall had in mind.

"We'll use Mr. Thersites office, shall we?" said Dr. Fall.

They took the elevator up to the executive floor.

Dr. Fall sniffed as they got out at the plush lobby. "Still haven't quite gotten rid of the mold, I see. Once that damp gets into the walls, it's the very Devil to get it out," he said conversationally.

They went into Thersites's office and Dr. Fall sat down behind the computer.

"Your copy, please."

Bogges handed him the story, and Dr. Fall turned on the computer.

"What about the rest of the paper?" asked Bogges.

"Oh, we'll just reprint yesterday's. No one will notice."

He began to type. Bogges thought it would be inaccurate to say that Dr. Fall's fingers flew across the keyboard. They were a blur. He finished in seconds.

"That was fifteen hundred words," said Bogges.

"On a good day, I do more than two thousand words a minute. I make a most efficient secretary, don't you think? Now, may I give you a ride home?"

"I think I'll walk."

"Suit yourself. I'll just stay here in case they have any questions at the plant."

"Look," said Bogges, "if you're doing this because you think it puts me under some obligation to you, forget it. I'm not taking you up on your offer."

"You may change your mind. In any event, I predict you'll be rather busy for the next few years. We'll be in touch."

Dr. Fall looked at Bogges expectantly. He wants me to ask him what he means, said Bogges to himself.

"Goodbye," said Bogges.

"Au revoir, Mr. Bogges."

Bogges hadn't gone a block from the office before the towering black poodle fell into step beside him. He sensed a companionable presence, although the dull red illumination cast by the creature's eyes on the sidewalk was surprising. They marched together quietly. Evidently the dog had sheathed its iron claws. Bogges was impressed by its courtesy. It was after three when Bogges unlocked his front door. During the last half hour of their way home, Bogges had begun to see stirrings of life: a garbage truck backing up to a dumpster, a brightly lit and empty bus that wouldn't stop for him, patrol cars prowling, a street cleaner. The spell had worn off. The dog left him when they turned onto his street. If Bogges had bothered to turn around he would have seen the poodle stop and gaze at him longingly. Bogges went to bed exhausted. Just before he fell asleep, he unplugged the phone from the outlet. There'd be plenty of time to resign later in the day without losing the rest of the night's sleep over it.

CHAPTER TWELVE

Bogges awoke at noon. Noises of malign import, thumpings, pound-
ings, bangings, and loud, angry voices at first suggested to him the
street was being torn up. Then it seemed to Bogges that the banging was
coming from inside the house. He realized that people, it sounded like a
multitude, were assaulting his door. He got out of bed and went to the
window, pushed it up, and leaned over the sill. Several dozen rough-looking men and one very rough-looking woman, all holding television cameras, along with a number of excessively groomed men and women with
microphones, had gathered around his front stoop and spilled onto the
sidewalk. Trucks with telescoping antennae and satellite dishes filled the
street from one end of the block to the other. At the sight of Bogges's bald-
ing head, the cameras aimed up. An animal roaring ascended. One roar
became articulate.

"So how does it feel to be the only man in Washington who's minding
his own business?"

A frightened look passed over Bogges's features. He jumped back from the window and slammed it shut. The assault on his door redoubled. He wanted to call Marina but the instant he plugged the phone back in it began ringing. He picked it up and a voice from the floor began interrogating him. He put a pillow over it and, feeling exposed in his own bedroom, took his clothes into the hallway to dress. The pounding on the door was only louder there. He heard a new note; a shuddering as though the door-frame was about to give way. He hurried into his clothes, went downstairs and out the back to the yard. The fence at the far end fronted an alley of old garages, brick walls and other fences in better general repair than Bogges's. The television mob hadn't yet penetrated to the alley. Bogges began to pull at the boards of his fence. They came away without protest, although one hollow with dry rot jaggedly split and filled his right hand with splinters. He squeezed into the space he had made and got stuck halfway. He pulled at another board and cried aloud when the waggling of his hips drove fresh splinters into his buttocks. In the final push to freedom, his pants caught on a nail and tore along the hem from thigh to ankle. With his trouser leg flapping, he waddled down the alley to the cross street. He stopped at the end of the alley and pressed his back against the wall. He craned his neck to peer around the corner. At this far end of the block there was one last television truck, its antennae extended two stories like, thought Bogges, a unicorn on Viagra. Two men guarding the truck looked at him with interest.

"Who the hell is that?" said one.

"Just some old bum sleeping it off in the alley."

Bogges took this as his cue. He came flapping down the street past the two men. The empty snap of his trousers made him realize he'd forgotten his wallet. He couldn't face another endless walk to the office.

"Could you spare a couple of bucks for the bus?" he said.

"It's only a dollar ten," said one of the men.

"I sure could use a dollar ten," said Bogges.

The man laughed and reached into his pocket. "Here, go get yourself a beer."

Bogges was tempted to take the advice, but then he'd have to walk. While he waited at the bus stop, he became aware of the state of his clothing. And just how do you have to dress, he asked himself, to quit your job? This fit of common-sense went some way to restoring his confidence. Still, he wished the breeze wouldn't blow like that against his exposed leg. He needed to pee.

■■■■■

Morrow-Graves was waiting by the guard post in the lobby of the paper.

"Mr. Thersites has been calling you every fifteen minutes since six a.m., Eustace. Where have you been?" Morrow-Graves spoke with more than customary anxiety.

"I have to pee, Lance."

"Mr. Thersites is waiting for you."

"Just let me go to the bathroom. Then he can fire me."

Morrow-Graves shook his head. "I'll just call up and say you're on your way."

"Fine."

In the elevator and down the hall to the men's room, reporters and columnists and editors and copy editors and copyboys and people from circulation and the business office and public relations drew aside as Bogges passed. Some of them looked at him eagerly; others cast their eyes down. Bogges had gotten used to being a minor pariah. This brisker notoriety was uncomfortable in a fresher and more unpleasant way. When he'd finished at the urinal, he thought he'd stare into the mirror for a while; this is what one is supposed to do at the great crossroads of life. But the sight of his unshaven muzzle changed his mind. Part of late middle age is not lingering before one's own image. He went straight up to the executive offices. Mr. Thersites's terrifying secretary—was her name Mrs. Basilisk? No, it couldn't be—glared at him.

"Mr. Thersites is expecting you," she said reprovingly.

"I know," said Bogges.

The glare became intermixed with shock at this presumption. Mrs. Ballistic—no, that wasn't right either—choked as she pronounced the next formula: "If you'll just take a seat, I'll see if Mr. Thersites is available."

Bogges couldn't resist. "But I thought you just said that Mr. Thersites was expecting me."

Before Mrs. Belle, Belletristic, Beale, Beelzebub, Buttocks, Ballocks, Balls, one of those, could respond, Thersites emerged from his lair.

"Good to see you, Eustace. Glad you could make it in."

Bogges thought the sarcasm, although characteristic of the Thersites style, was unnecessary. "Look, I know I'm finished as the Letters editor, but I did the best I could last night. I thought it was important to get the paper out, even if it was mostly the same paper as the day before. Anyway," Bogges was babbling, "it wasn't my fault that everyone decided that minding your own business meant leaving work and going home. Well, I guess it was my fault because I printed that letter, but you can't hold me responsible for how things turned out."

Mr. Thersites stared at Bogges blankly. "I don't know what you're talking about, Eustace. Although you're right that you're finished as the Letters editor. Mrs. Balsam," he said to his secretary, "is it true that the paper, aside from Eustace's story, was the same as the day before?

"I really can't say, Mr. Thersites. I'll look into it right away."

"Don't bother," said Thersites. "If someone notices, I'm sure I'll hear about it."

Then he led Bogges into his office and shut the door.

"Can I get you a drink, Eustace? You look like you had a hard night."

"Yes, please."

Thersites went over to a lacquered credenza, pulled out a drawer, and pushed up a sort of cover or hood. A flap in the front of the drawer went down to reveal a small bar. Bogges watched him pour a brownish liquid into two heavy crystal glasses, thinking that this almost made being fired pleasant. He wondered why Thersites was bothering to make it pleasant. Maybe he found it difficult to fire people. This wasn't plausible. Thersites handed Bogges his glass, went around his desk, and sat.

"Sit, Eustace."

Bogges obediently sat. The splinters reminded him not to shift in his chair.

"I fired"—Thersites pronounced the name of the managing editor—"this morning. If it had been up to the publisher, you could have had my job, but I'm only eleven months from retirement. I made him see that the litigation would run on longer than the remainder of my contract. You'll probably feel more comfortable after a little seasoning in the number-two job anyway. Do you think three thirty-eight will be acceptable? Of course with the options, it's worth closer to twice that, and next year, when I'm gone, you can negotiate your own deal."

Bogges took care not to gulp. "Three hundred and thirty-eight thousand dollars?"

"That's what your predecessor was making. But I see your point. I'm authorized to offer you up to four fifty. After that, we have to talk to the owners."

The unreality of the situation rendered Bogges hysterical. "Four hundred and fifty would be fine," he said with an idiot giggle.

"I imagine you'll want to make some changes around here," said Thersites.

Bogges was still working to suppress his giggle; the timing of this last remark was disastrous. He tried to say change, but change became a chuckle which became in turn a stuttering cha cha cha. Bogges's broad mouth widened and gaped and the laughter poured out and no air came in and his diaphragm became knotted under the strain and he began to choke. His face was red and he might have died of suffocation if Thersites hadn't pounded him on the back.

"We're even," said Thersites at the end of the crisis. "Especially since I've never liked you."

"I've never liked you either," gasped Bogges.

Thersites snorted. It made him look more human. "I've also never liked the paper," he confessed.

"Me too."

"So what do you have in mind for it?"

Bogges tried to control his breathing. "Don't you think the problem is the paper's 'personality'? Wouldn't it be more likeable, or at least there'd be less to dislike, if we got rid of the shrill, high-pitched voices and the low, pontificating ones and the even-toned but fundamentally self-righteous persona in the middle that's supposed to signify balance?"

Thersites began laughing and, at the same time, started to look almost completely human. "Should we fire all the columnists? We could do it together!"

"And the editors," said Bogges, regaining breath and enthusiasm.

Thersites looked troubled. "But who would write the stories?"

"We could teach the reporters to write," said Bogges.

"The owners would like that," said Thersites thoughtfully. "It would be a cost-savings. We might get a raise."

"I just got a raise," said Bogges.

"You could get another."

"I think I'd miss Lance," said Bogges.

"Who's that?" asked Thersites.

"He's the Assistant Managing Editor in charge of Science, Religion, Obits, and Letters."

"Oh, yeah, the odds-and-ends guy. Look, anything you decide to do is jake with me. I'm going to lunch." Thersites looked happy at the thought of lunch. Then his face fell. "I suppose you want to go to lunch with me."

"Thanks, but I have a lot to do."

Thersites's face cleared. "Some other time then. See you around. Let me know how you're getting on, what you're up to, you know."

"Sure."

Thersites got up to go to lunch. He halted while still rounding the desk. "I think you should leave first, Eustace. This is my office."

"Right."

On his way down to the newsroom, Bogges began composing a memo in his head to the columnists: Insofar as you are expected to draw conclusions from fact, you enjoy more freedom than reporters. However, if you do not make the facts your own, your opinions are by definition second-hand. Therefore, you will depend on your own reporting for the facts you muster in support of your opinions. The emphasis of this paper's opinion writers will now bear on original reporting. Any columnist who remains dependent on the opinions of so-called opinion leaders or what he reads in the paper instead of what he discovers for himself on the ground ... Yes, something along those lines. A good half dozen of the prima donnas should quit by the end of the day without Bogges having to lift a finger. The part about what he discovers for himself should be sufficient to terminally insult the ancient female columnist known as Herself. He wondered if he could do the same to the editorial-page writers. No, they belonged to the owners. Perhaps he could convince the owners that controversy sparks interest, and since the paper would be emphasizing fact ... Of course, the marketing people had trained the owners to avoid controversy by eliminating uncomfortable facts. They called it embracing diversity.

When the elevator doors opened at the news floor, Bogges was met by the editors of National, Foreign, Metro, and the former managing editor's secretary.

"We'll have White House reaction to yesterday's demonstrations in an hour," said National.

"The French are interpreting yesterday's events as a decision to shorten the work week. They are applauding what they call the newfound American recognition of the human need for leisure," said Foreign.

"The mayor is worried about tax receipts in the District," said Metro.

"I have forty-five requests for interviews, Mr. Bogges," said the secretary, "not including the networks."

"Journalists interviewing journalists," said Bogges, "is like the Ouijee bird. It flies around in ever-diminishing concentric circles until finally it disappears up its own ... You know what I mean, Vicki," remembering the secretary's name.

"Should I tell them that they're all assholes?" asked Vicki.

"I'll leave it up to you. I look forward to working with you."

"I do too, Mr. Bogges."

"We should lead with the White House," said National.

"And make the French the off-lead," said Foreign.

"We'll thrash it out at the story conference," replied Bogges, thinking he'd bury both stories. "How many reporters do you have asking people what they thought they were doing yesterday?" he asked Metro.

"I've got five. It's all I could spare," said Metro.

"OK, borrow a dozen more from National and Life and Styles. Vicki, ask JT to come to my office in fifteen minutes, would you. I have a call to make first."

"Yes, Mr. Bogges."

Bogges made his way to the managing editor's glass-walled office in the corner of the newsroom. Reporters and copy editors in their tens and dozens stopped typing, put down phones, closed their mouths in mid conversation. Some stood to get a better view. Bogges arranged his features to evoke a stern and determined mien. He tried to adjust his elephantine waddle to a stately progress. This at least stopped his trouser leg from flapping. He passed by the Religion desk. An idea occurred to him, and he forgot all about his dignity.

"Listen," he said to the editor, "isn't there some theologian at Georgetown who performs exorcisms?"

"There's a Jesuit on the faculty," said Religion, "who was an advisor on the set of the Exorcist movie. I don't know if he actually performs exorcisms."

"That's the one. Send someone to interview him or better yet, go yourself. Ask him what he thinks was going on yesterday. See if he thinks the Devil was involved."

"You want this for the Saturday Religion page?"

"No. We'll put it on the front page tomorrow below the fold."

"I haven't been on the front page since the pope was elected."

"Oh, well," said Bogges. "Come in later and we'll talk about those bureaus you wanted in the Vatican and Jerusalem. Maybe we should shut down the Paris bureau and send him to Rome. Any chance of getting someone into Mecca?"

Religion laughed. "I'll look into it. By the way, congratulations, Eustace."

"Thanks." Then Bogges began laughing too. "We'll try to have some fun before they fire me, shall we?"

"Your wish is my command, exalted one."

Abel Japrowski met Bogges at the door to his new office. "Shares are up. Wall Street analysts seem to think it's because Washington shut down yesterday and couldn't do any mischief to free markets."

"Those analysts are really full of crap, aren't they?" said Bogges.

"Yes."

"Write it that way."

"With pleasure. I'm sorry about what happened between us, Eustace."

"Forget it. Anyway, I was sleepwalking."

"It didn't feel like that when you shoved me."

"I'd like you and Miriam to meet my friend Marina. How about dinner Saturday?"

"It's a date. You know, I think that your being made managing editor is one of those miracles that make you believe there is a God."

"I don't think God had anything to do with it, Abel. But thanks."

Bogges shut the door of his office and surveyed the territory. He walked over to the excessively large desk, remembered it was used for story conferences among the editors, and looked at the buttons on the telephone. He picked it up and pushed the button marked Vicki.

"Would you have someone bring my typewriter. It's in the Letters office."

"I'll get it myself, Mr. Bogges."

"No, it's heavy. Send a copyboy."

"A news-aide," she corrected.

Bogges decided to save that battle for another day without for a moment conceding that this wasn't a battle worth fighting. "Fine, thanks," he said.

He examined the buttons on the telephone again and pushed one that wasn't marked. Then he tried another. When he got a dial tone, he rang Marina's restaurant.

"We're in the middle of lunch," said whoever answered. "I'm sorry, but Marina is too busy in the kitchen to come to the phone. May I take a message?"

"Just tell her Eustace Bogges called and I'll try her later."

"Oh, Mr. Bogges. Marina said to tell her if you called. Please hold."

While he waited, Bogges listened to the noises of the restaurant. His belly rumbled. He wondered how he was going to get lunch. Then Marina's breathy voice came on the line.·

"We're so busy, I can only talk a minute. You're famous, Eustace. Imagine, the only journalist who did his duty. I'm very, very proud of you."

"I want to see you. I need to talk to you."

"Can you come in at the end of lunch?"

"Well, no. I think I'll have to be here until about seven, when the first edition is put to bed."

"Why do you have to stay so late?"

"I've been appointed managing editor."

Then Bogges took the phone away so that Marina's cries weren't right in his ear. He waited until he could make out the restaurant noises again.

"Oh, Eustace, I can hardly believe it."

"I can hardly believe it too. Look, I'll come in for dinner and we'll talk after. Oh hell, I'm not dressed or shaved."

'You went to work in your nightshirt?"

"No, no, it's a long story. I'll have to go home and clean up. Can you come over?

"I can leave at nine o'clock if things are quiet."

"Then I'll see you at my place around nine-thirty."

Lunch had become an urgent matter. He'd just have time to go outside to the half-smoke vendor. He was about to get up from his chair, leather, very comfortable, easy on splintered rumps, when he saw JT peering through the glass wall of the office. JT's expression was belligerent, with elements of resentment and fear. It made him look like a child. He is a child, thought Bogges. He felt obliged to take care of him. Bogges bellowed, "Come in."

JT came in defiantly. How, Bogges asked himself, does one come in defiantly? He supposed it was a combination of hesitance and aggression, but that didn't quite solve it.

"Sit down." Bogges gestured at one of the low chairs on the other side of the desk.

JT sat; his chin was barely above the edge of the desk. Bogges restrained himself from offering JT a phone book as a booster.

"I need your help."

JT looked warily at Bogges. "Why? I mean, how? I mean, how can I help?"

The wariness was still there, but so was something else: hope or calculation. Perhaps they were, to JT, the same thing.

"You watch TV, don't you?"

"Of course I do. Everyone does." JT couldn't quite manage to hide his annoyance, his contempt for Bogges's query.

"Not everyone. I do not." Bogges spoke kindly, with an avuncular benignity. After all, he was dealing with a child. He reminded himself he must be careful not to make the child cry. "But I saw some the other night, something about two girls and dating and being engaged and blow jobs. Then there was an ad for something women use that I didn't know about."

"Sure, that was *Eat Me*, the top-rated show in the country, worldwide. You see," said JT eagerly, "we've all been waiting to see whether Janet could stay faithful to Bob, that's her fiancé, when she went out with Harry, that's her old boyfriend who she's still hot for. Well, in a surprising twist, she sort of did stay faithful, but, in a way, she didn't. *Eat Me* is sponsored by Pneumatica. Women use it for dryness."

"Why don't they just get a drink?" asked Bogges. "That's what I do."

JT looked at Bogges as though he were mad, or from another planet. "You're kidding."

Bogges realized they were getting off the track. "Sure," he said, pleased with his command of the vernacular. "Look, what do you think of *TV Week*?"

This was the Sunday insert that listed the following week's offerings on television.

"What do I think of it? It carries what's on. It's a service."

"It's a service," repeated Bogges quietly. His tone of voice suggested he'd never heard such wisdom so brilliantly epitomized. "But," he said, "what about the people who have difficulty following the plots? And what about the people who find the ads too allusive? What about them? Are we serving them?"

"No, I guess not. But anyone who can't follow a TV show probably can't read the paper either."

Bogges thought he could overcome this dilemma. "I experience no trouble reading the paper."

"No, I didn't mean you. I was trying to say that—"

Bogges cut him off. "I know what you're trying to say. You want to expand our coverage, because more is better."

"Sure."

"You want to give our readers more than a mere TV schedule."

"Sure."

"Because that would be better."

"Sure."

"And you have a good idea about how we can do that, right?"

A somewhat tentative "Sure."

"You want us"—Bogges paused on a rising note—"to summarize the plots for them!"

JT nodded his head. Then he shook it. His head wobbled. "But if we tell them what's going to happen in the next episode, why would they bother to watch?"

This was an excellent question. The answer might be that people would stop wasting their time in front of the TV. For some reason, Bogges thought all was now in God's hands. "You wouldn't want to buy something without knowing what it was, would you?"

"No, of course not," said JT.

"And," continued Bogges, "that's why you think we should explain the ads. So our subscribers can decide for themselves if they actually want what they are being solicited to buy."

"I guess that makes sense."

"But if we don't want our subscribers to buy something without knowing what it is, how can we ask them to watch something without knowing what's going to happen?"

JT seemed to be thinking this proposition over. He became enthused. "We could, we could bring the news to TV viewing," he said. "We could transform the way that the consumer, the American public, watches."

"Remarkable," said Bogges.

"We could rename the insert, make it a must-read in the Sunday paper." JT took a deep breath, launched his blockbuster. "We could call it *Heads-Up TV*."

Bogges smiled indulgently. "That is certainly a startling notion. Where do you think Sally would fit in?"

"She'd be brilliant interpreting the ads."

"Put her right on it," said Bogges.

"The way I see this, Eustace, is a whole new concept. I think we'll need to make the insert a glossy."

Bogges pretended to look concerned. "I'm not sure about the budget." This was accurate. Bogges had no idea about budgets. He pulled at his lower lip. "I'd like to find the money for you, JT. But where?"

Both men sighed.

Bogges now pretended to suddenly have an idea. "I have an idea. You're going to have your hands full with *Heads-Up TV*. I'll let the assistant editors look after Books and Life and Styles while you're busy, ah, refining your, ah, concept. Of course, this will mean a slight reduction in your salary, while you're working on the project, but once it's off and running, well, who knows what the future might hold?"

"I can't accept a cut."

"I don't think the owners would look kindly on someone who was unwilling to meet new challenges."

"How big a cut?"

"Just enough to pay for slick covers."

"We could stay with pulp."

"No, JT. That's very generous, but I don't want a mere question of money to limit your, ah, vision."

"You think the owners are serious?"

"They might want to make you a wholly owned subsidiary."

JT drew himself up. His face was rapt. "We could go head-to-head with *TV Guide*."

"Think of that," said Bogges. "I'm going outside to get a half-smoke. Want to join me?"

JT tried to control his features. Half-smokes were not the sort of thing he cared to put into his system. He got up. "Thanks, I'll take a raincheck. I've got a lot on my plate. I think I'll need a bigger TV in my office, you know, a split screen so that I can watch more than one show at a time."

"No," said Bogges.

The half-smoke steam cart had vanished by the time Bogges finally got downstairs. He set off toward the oyster bar. A quick couple of dozen and a carafe of white should see him through the story conference at 3:00. He realized it was 3:00. He turned back with a curse. He poked his head into Vicki's cubicle before going to his desk.

"I'm starving," he said faintly.

"There's coffee and cookies in the women's lounge. Or would you rather I run out to McDonald's?"

Bogges gulped. A man had to draw the line somewhere. "Coffee and cookies would be wonderful."

Vicki brought a substantial platter. Half an hour later, Bogges was working on the crumbs. National was still trying to get onto the front page.

"We've got time to do an investigative piece on this Chakravarti character," said National.

Everyone at the table knew this wasn't possible.

"You won't find him," said Bogges. "Anyway, you can't conduct an investigation. Newspapers don't have subpoena powers. You can conduct an inquiry. No, that's wrong too. You can make inquiries. But, as regards Chakravarti, you'll just have to take my word for it that it's a waste of time."

National was not at all ready to take Bogges's word for this. He glanced at Foreign and looked down at his notes. Bogges sensed a conspiracy germinating. He decided not to make himself ridiculous by giving it another thought.

"So, Metro will have the lead with the hard-news follow-up and the off-lead with man-on-the-street reaction," said Bogges. "We'll put Religion below the fold, and, unless something changes between now and seven o'clock, we'll let Business fill up the middle. Any questions?"

There were no questions. Metro shot out of his seat. He had work to do. Abel Japrowski also left with dispatch. He hadn't been on the front page since the market last crashed. Foreign and National got up with the lack of urgency that befitted their positions. Lance Morrow-Graves lingered. Religion wasn't back yet, and, in any event, he'd be doing all the real work.

"I did the letters, Eustace."

Bogges was stricken. He'd forgotten about the page. "Thank you, Lance. I guess we need to hire someone."

"If it's alright with you, Eustace, I'd like to keep doing it. You see, I think it's rather interesting."

At this point, Morrow-Graves seemed to lose his English accent. "You know, Science and Religion and Obits are really good. The truth is, they don't need supervision. You've all been nice, very tolerant, but I get in the way, so I try not to interfere. The real truth is that I don't have much to do here, except hold meetings that no one wants to go to. I like Letters. I like finding out what people are thinking and helping them say it more clearly."

"Of course you can keep Letters, Lance."

"I suppose you won't need an assistant managing editor in charge of odds and ends anymore?"

Bogges looked surprised.

Lance gave a self-deprecating smile. "Yes, I know what they call me upstairs."

"It does seem like a silly title," said Bogges.

"It was a silly position," said Morrow-Graves. "I'm glad not to feel silly anymore. What?"

Until Morrow-Graves had tied up this particular loose end, Bogges hadn't had time to realize there were loose ends to tie up. He now thought of Robinson, the man who had saved him from having to give up his Hermes for a flat screen. He wondered how he might repay him for his years of help avoiding computers. Bogges was about to ask Vicki to invite him to his office but decided this was not the sort of managing editor he was going to be.

"Vicki, I'm going to talk to Robinson. I'll be back in a few minutes."

Robinson was looking particularly unkempt.

"So, you sold out," he said when Bogges entered his cubicle.

"I hope not, Robinson. I have been trying very hard the last couple of weeks not to sell out. Time will tell, I suppose. Is there anything I can do for you?"

In answer, Robinson swiveled his chair around and showed Bogges the back of his head. Bogges smiled, saluted the head and returned to his office.

By 6:30 nothing had happened to change the makeup of the front page. Bogges puttered around until 6:55, finding a pint of whiskey in one drawer and explicit magazines in another. He toasted his predecessor with the whiskey. Vicki was still in her cubicle.

"Why are you here?" asked Bogges on his way out.

"You haven't given me leave to go."

"In the future," said Bogges, "you go when you're ready and not a second after."

"Thank you. I've called a cab."

"Thanks."

"I didn't think any would stop for you," she said.

Bogges remembered his pants. "I'll try to look better tomorrow."

"I think you look fine."

"You're a terrible liar. Good night."

It was on the tip of Bogges's tongue to ask Vicki about Pneumatica, but some instinct prevented him. Feeling very much the managing editor, Bogges interviewed the cab driver on his ride home.

"Pretty unusual, what happened yesterday," said Bogges.

"Think so?"

"Well, yes, everyone leaving work in the middle of the day, milling around in the streets, demanding that people mind their own business. This sort of thing doesn't happen all the time."

"People are a bunch of assholes. What'd you expect? I didn't make a dime after two o'clock."

Bogges then asked him to turn on the radio. When Bogges was home he went downstairs to the kitchen and got out hotdogs and sauerkraut. As he put them in a pot he remembered that he must buy caraway seeds the next time he went to the market. While they were stewing, he went up to shave, shower, and dress. When he returned to the front parlor, he found Dr. Fall mixing martinis.

"What are you doing here?" asked Bogges. "Never mind. Get out."

"I'll be leaving shortly. Here."

Dr. Fall handed Bogges a glass. He was dressed in a black suit, well worn, shiny at the elbows and knees, a headwaiter's outfit, or an undertaker's.

Bogges drank. The thought of Marina encountering Dr. Fall was intolerable. "I want you to go now."

"I'll be long gone before Marina arrives," said Dr. Fall. "But first, we have some unfinished business to attend to."

Bogges put his glass down. He wondered briefly how it could remain frosted after being handled. He wasn't surprised that it was still full. He found he didn't want any more of it. "We have no unfinished business, because we have no further business," said Bogges carefully.

"Something's come up, Eustace." Dr. Fall spoke the name affectionately.

Bogges realized it was the first time he'd been addressed this way. The use of his first name seemed deadly serious. "What's come up?"

"Your time."

"I beg your pardon."

"Your time is up."

"What do you mean my time is up?" asked Bogges, knowing exactly what it meant.

"I'm sorry," said Dr. Fall.

"You're sorry?"

"This isn't what I'd planned."

"You said last night that I would be busy for the next few years."

Dr. Fall shrugged. "As you know, I don't always call the shots."

"You've come to kill me, but you're only following orders, right? It's not your fault."

Dr. Fall shook his head. "No, that's the Angel of Death's job. I sow. When the soil is fertile, I harvest the fruits of my labor. Sometimes, my crop is expropriated."

"But why?" Bogges was pleased that his voice didn't break.

"Who knows? Perhaps He likes the paper the way it is."

"He's a subscriber?"

"Well, of course, on Sundays He gets the *Times*."

Bogges sat down in the little green armchair that fitted him like a glove. "It's that *Heads-Up TV* insert. This is JT's doing," he muttered.

"It doesn't have to be this way," said Dr. Fall. "I can give you more time."

Bogges looked up. "You can?"

"Yes. As long as you want. I mean, as long as you want within the customary span. You can be the managing editor, next year the executive editor. You will marry Marina. Tonight, you can make love to her."

"Mind your own business," Bogges snapped.

Dr. Fall was abashed. "Forgive me. But I can give you more time."

Time, life, Bogges was filled with yearning for both, also for Marina, the paper, hot dogs and sauerkraut. "What's to become of me?" he sighed.

"You will die."

Bogges again sighed. It was hard not to look woebegone. He forced himself to speak. "Then what?"

Dr. Fall twinkled. "You mean compared to Marina, the paper, hot dogs and sauerkraut? Compared to those things, my poor friend, an emptiness. Of course, you're confusing categories again."

"Which categories?"

"Life and death."

Bogges gave up pursuing this line of inquiry for the last time. "What do I have to do?" he asked.

"The usual bargain."

"What is the usual bargain?"

"Come, come, Eustace, you know what's required."

"Why won't you tell me?"

"Do you really want it spelled out?" asked Dr. Fall. "Every i dotted and every t crossed, I promise this, that, and such and so in exchange for your signature, on parchment, in letters that flame as they are written, and then, while the world holds its breath, the document is consumed in thunder and smoke, and with a sulfurous blast, filed in Hell, the true Faustian contract, is that what you want?"

"I want to see what's in that contract," said Bogges.

"Really, there's no need. Your word is good enough for me."

"And if I give you my word?"

"Then you will have being-in-time. You will have now."

"You sound just like Chakravarti, another phony."

"That is a very reductive way of looking at the matter," said Dr. Fall.

But to Bogges, dying seemed like a very reductive way of looking at the matter. He wasn't ready; he had the necessary and urgent acts of life to perform: work and love, eating and drinking. He'd never been so hungry. He felt that he was finally exercising his faculties after a lifetime of sleepwalking. He thought that Dr. Fall's stories, from Eve to the present, must have been part of that sleepwalking, dreams before waking, or all one long dream that was a tremendous longing to be awake. He felt that he had begun to see only now how to mind his own business. With this realization, he looked up to see Dr. Fall silently leave the house. He'd left the door ajar, but Bogges couldn't now be bothered to get up from his chair and close it after him. It was a mercy that the chair was so comfortable. He hardly felt the splinters in his rump.

Rumple roast, thought Bogges hungrily before he drifted off.

Marina was late. Encumbered by a tray of food, she rang Bogges's doorbell with the point of her elbow. She waited, then rang again. The tray pushed against the door, and it swung open. Marina entered. Bogges seemed to be asleep in his chair. She set the tray down carefully on the mail table and looked tenderly at the peaceful figure. She thought he had the calm and mild regard of a sleeping infant, well, infant hippo. No, he was not handsome. But there was undeniable appeal, like certain dogs whose peculiar features are nevertheless more expressive than obvious good looks.

She sniffed. Something was burning. She'd let him sleep while she saw to whatever disaster he'd left down in the kitchen. But first, she'd give him a kiss. She leaned over and pressed her lips against his. Bogges didn't stir. He hardly appeared to be breathing. Marina sighed. Without admitting it to herself, she had wanted him to awake with a smile to her kiss. She looked again at the unconscious figure. She suddenly insisted that he wake to her kiss. She demanded it. She put her mouth on his. But his lips were dry, and oddly cold. How dare he sleep when she wanted him awake, and tonight of all nights when, she felt sure, they would seal their bargain in love. She pressed harder. She breathed her own breath into him. But Bogges was dead to the world. It was intolerable. Marina shook him.

"Wake up, Eustace!" she commanded.

For a moment, the fierce woman stood over the inanimate man. Then Bogges opened his eyes in astonishment, and all of Marina's fierceness melted away.